In Love's Own Time

In Love's Own Time

Book One
of the Enduring Faith Series

SUSAN C. FELDHAKE

ZondervanPublishingHouse
Grand Rapids, Michigan
A Division of HarperCollinsPublishers

In Love's Own Time
Copyright © 1984 by Susan C. Feldhake

Reprinted as Book One of the Enduring Faith Series in 1993

Requests for information should be addressed to:
Zondervan Publishing House
Grand Rapids, Michigan 49530

Library of Congress Cataloging in Publication Data

Feldhake, Susan C.
    In love's own time / Susan C. Feldhake
        p.   cm. – (Enduring faith series : bk. 1)
    ISBN 0-310-48111-2
    I. Title. II. Series: Feldhake, Susan C. Enduring faith series : bk. 1.
PS3556.E4575I5   1993
813'.54—dc20   92-33214
                                                                    CIP

Edited by Anne Severance
Cover design by Jody Langley
Cover illustration by Jim Spoelstra

Printed in the United States of America

93 94 95 96 97 98 99 00 01 / LP / 10 9 8 7 6 5 4 3 2 1

*In deep appreciation
to the citizens of Effingham County, Illinois,
past and present
who made this area all that it is today . . .
a good place to call home*

chapter

1

SUE ELLEN STONE sighed and pressed her back into the plush cushions of the train seat, squinting against the black soot that belched from the locomotive chugging south across the plains of central Illinois. The April noon sun soared high to shorten the dark shadow that scurried over the grass beside the train as it snorted along the ribbon of rail.

Already she and her son, Jeremiah, had encountered a few folks from the general region, exchanging amused glances upon hearing the twanging accents and unfamiliar patterns of speech. Still, she had been touched by the friendliness of these good people, and believing that there would be a haven for them in the state that would soon be their new home, her spirits lifted.

At least, Sue Ellen sincerely *hoped*, she and Jem would be accepted by their new neighbors, just as the recently widowed woman and her son were prepared to accept others exactly as they were. The accents might be different, the educational backgrounds too, but they were all human beings, after all, with the same basic needs, feelings, and desires. Such common emotions would surely unite them in the face of any surface diversities.

Several cars ahead of her coach, the Illinois Central

engineer yanked the cord. Sue Ellen winced, stiffening with the throaty bellow warning of the train's approach to the crossroad.

She peered out at the long amber grass towering over lush green sprouts. The grass bent, tangling into tight eddies under the tormenting current as the train streaked by. Then once more the grass lay tranquil.

"Your stop's coming up, ma'am," the conductor said, giving Sue Ellen a cheerful smile. "You might want to wake your boy."

Twelve-year-old Jeremiah Stone cracked one eye open for an instant before it drooped shut again.

When the train began to slow at the edge of town, Sue Ellen tugged at his sleeve. "Jem, we're almost there," she whispered, then smiled. Her son's tousled dark hair was so like his father's, his frame leaner and lankier than most boys his age.

All morning the land had been flat for as far as the eye could see—its openness broken only by occasional fencerows and clumps of hickory, oak, or soft maple, which gave pause to dark patches of newly worked sod.

Sue Ellen's pulse quickened when the train halted before the peeling depot. A weather-faded sign proclaimed their destination: *Effingham, Illinois!*

With a grating clash of steel against steel, the train shuddered to a halt.

"Effingham! Check your stop!" the conductor bawled.

The man paced the aisle, craning left and right, routing sleepy travelers who had chosen the county seat as their destination. A few, their journeys uncompleted, nestled against the seat to witness mutely the flurry of activity on the platform parallel to depot and tracks.

"This is it, Jem. We're almost home," Sue Ellen breathed with relief.

The boy, lulled to lethargy by days of riding the rhythmic rails, nodded with excitement, helpless to stifle an eager grin. Jem picked up their hand luggage and bounded from the car, his slim, sedate mother in his wake. Railroad workers had already unloaded the trunk from the baggage car.

The heat of the late April sun burning down on Sue Ellen Stone's black mourning dress almost took her breath away. She swayed dizzily from the warm blast, reeling from its contrast to the gentle breezes of the vast northland she'd left behind in Minnesota.

"All aboooaaard!" the conductor bellowed. "All aboard!"

The uniformed man glanced around. Seeing no new passengers, he scooped up the squatty stool and hopped into the rail car. Leaning out, he clung to the handrail and waved the engineer on.

Jem flicked at a pesky fly circling his face. "What do we do now, Ma?"

Sue Ellen gave him a bright smile that hid her sudden surge of confusion.

"Why—we go to our new home! That is, just as soon as I can inquire about renting a wagon." She glanced about, frowning when she saw the brick hotel a block away but no livery stable nearby and no parked wagon on the street with a driver for hire. "Surely the depot agent will know someone who can take us the rest of the way."

Jem plunked himself down on the trunk to wait while Sue Ellen strolled into the cool, dim building.

The agent looked up from his telegraph key. "Can I help you, ma'am?" he drawled.

"My son and I need transportation to our farm on Salt

Creek," she explained. "I expected to find someone I could pay to take us there."

The clerk nodded. "Ordinarily there would be someone, ma'am, but not today. Sam's off on a haulin' job. He won't be back until morning. Figgered he'd better take the job—'cause most days he meets the train and drives away without a single passenger."

"Tomorrow morning?" Sue Ellen repeated in a faint voice. She thought of her dwindling funds, more precious now that their destination was still miles away. "I—I'm afraid I can't wait that long."

The depot agent shrugged. "If you're in a hurry, then I suggest you make other arrangements. You might be able to hail a passin' wagon—if you're lucky."

Smiling her thanks, Sue Ellen nodded and stepped outside to face Jem's expectant gaze. She spoke before he could voice his question.

"There's no wagon today," she said and repeated the agent's advice. "You stay with the trunk, Jem. I'll see if I can find a driver who'll haul us to our farm."

Jem tugged his hat brim over his eyes and stared down the gleaming iron rails that twinkled in the sun until they merged and disappeared into the distance. Sue Ellen stiffened her back and marched with determination to Banker Street where the road jogged south across the Pennsylvania Railroad tracks that divided the town into north and south, intersecting with the Illinois Central rails at the depot.

Several people strolling by, exchanged pleasantries as they assessed the widow, a stranger to their town. Sue Ellen's polite responses were uttered from habit. In her state of mind she could think of little else but how to solve the problem of getting to their farm.

Sue Ellen heaved a sigh when a nattily dressed rider passed

by on his expensive saddle horse. With his riding crop tucked neatly under his arm, he tipped his hat to her and proceeded north. The horse's hooves clacked on the red brick street. Minutes later, a ragged peddler with a mule-drawn wagon rolled north without comment.

"Oh, dear!" Sue Ellen fretted and chewed her lip as she looked quickly around. Traffic to the south was discouragingly absent, and the oppressive heat enveloped her like a heavy quilt, smothering her to drowsiness. She tried not to think about the precious time flitting by.

Sue Ellen was unsure how long she had alternately stood in the shade of a sweet gum tree and paced the hot street. She wondered if she'd been dozing on her feet when she was startled by a racket that clamored terrifyingly close yet was too far away for her to recognize.

Claps, clanks, creaks, and banshee-like groans pierced the air. Her heart hammering with fright, Sue Ellen rushed toward the side of the street to avoid the source of the noise, which, from the volume of it, was just around a bend in the street.

Instinctively Sue Ellen glanced toward Jem to assure herself of his safety. She saw him, lulled almost to sleep beneath the scorching sun. The sharp crack of a whip, which caused her to start with alarm, was not lost on Jem. Shaken, he sprang from the trunk, whirling as his worried eyes sought the direction of the confounding commotion.

Their eyes met for an instant. Sue Ellen saw Jem's mouth drop open to form a horrified O and then she turned, her eyes widening with terror, as a team of sweat-flecked, snorting Clydesdales thundered blindly toward the railroad crossing.

"Ma! Watch out, Ma!" Jem's voice trailed off in a thin, agonized wail.

Sue Ellen pinched her eyes shut, expecting at any instant to be trampled and battered beneath the stomping hooves. The huge draft horses passed so close she could feel her skirt swirl. Even when she realized that the danger had brushed past, her eyes remained tightly closed, not from fright but in thankful prayer for her deliverance.

The moment of relief was broken by a hoarse stream of vile words, some of which she didn't recognize. From the inflection, however, the meaning was clear.

Sue Ellen, her face drained ashen, peered up at a giant of a man. The swarthy, darkly bearded six-footer, with broad shoulders straining at the seams of his faded shirt, narrowed his piercing blue eyes and glared at Sue Ellen from his towering perch.

The sleek, spirited horses bobbed their heads and snorted impatiently, pawing the road until their harness bells tinkled. Foam frothed their velvety muzzles and their chestnut brown hides were dark with sweat from the hard run.

"Move aside and let me pass, lady!" the man ordered as his curses gave way to intelligible speech. "It's some kind of foolishness standin' in the middle of the road that way. If it's run over you want, before the day's over someone's sure to oblige you where Alton Wheeler won't. Now move!"

Sue Ellen's lips formed a grim line as a flush suffused her neck and face. She was tired and hot from the long journey. But above all, she was disappointed. Ordinarily a genteel woman, Sue Ellen was in no mood to be bullied by a rough-talking, rude stranger. Words as sharp as his own boiled in her mind. She clenched her fists to wrest control. Then swallowing hard, she spoke, but her words were as deliberately mild as his had been harsh.

"I'm sorry to inconvenience you, sir," she apologized. "I didn't intend to get in your way. I was only trying to hire a wagon to take my son and me to our farm."

The man growled a curt response and dropped back into the wagon seat as if his legs threatened to give way. He raised his strong wrists to snap the leather reins across the backs of the matched team, a gelding and a stallion. Sue Ellen stepped aside, turned in a swirl of black skirts, and started for the platform where Jem waited.

Uncomfortably aware of the angry stranger's blue eyes burning into her back, she refused to turn and confront his impudent gaze but walked on, listening for the snap of reins and the jingle of harness bells that would signal his departure. Only silence greeted her ears.

The wagonmaster fingered the soft, worn leather reins and waited for his crazily beating heart to slow. He stared after the slight woman—no bigger than a mite, she was—with shiny black hair that curled where it strayed in wisps from the neat coronet of braids around her head. Flashing before his eyes was the image of her terrified features, which had kindled his own fright and left him weak and shaky in the knees as he waited for the agonized screams and the thud and lurch of the buckboard passing over her body.

He blinked, reassuring himself that she was indeed alive and unscathed. Her stricken face, however, was branded in his memory. Something—he couldn't say just what—was different about this woman.

Crude as he was, Alton slowly realized that the look on her pretty face was not merely an expression of fear but of a far deeper wounding. *That's it!* he thought. His *words* had offended her. As the idea registered, he cursed himself for being a clumsy oaf. He'd been raised better and, though he'd strayed far from his godly roots, Alton Wheeler had been taught manners and decency.

Now, just because this woman had scared him witless, was no excuse to rail at her like a madman in his wild relief that she was not dead beneath his wagon wheels. He knew from the stiff, proud set of her back beneath the faded widow's weeds that she was aching with hurt, and he sensed that a torrent of tears was just a breath away. If so, they were his to claim, because he'd treated her like she was the kind of woman she was obviously *not*.

Alton thought back over his thirty-three years—a lifetime that had taken him across the plains, up and down the length of the Mississippi River on a barge, and in and out of more saloon doors than he cared to remember. In all that time he'd never deliberately hurt anyone—gambling partner or painted bargirl. He must make amends.

But how? he wondered now. Were the woman a barroom floozy, it would have been an easy matter to make her smile. But the last thing he wanted to do was approach this—this *lady* and make matters even worse.

Alton massaged his temples as he thought, squinting against the crashing headache wrought by too much strong liquor in combination with the penetrating glare of sunlight.

Dully, Alton stared at the broad rumps of the horses he'd won in a backroom poker game at the Idle Hour Saloon in St. Louis the week before.

For a moment Alton considered driving on and forcing the bothersome incident from his mind, but he knew that the memory of the hurt in those green eyes would haunt him. No! If nothing else, he was at least an honest man, and he played fair and square—whether the game be cards or women.

Abruptly the tall teamster leaped from the wagon. He cleared his throat, and when neither the widow nor her son acknowledged his approach, he was tempted to turn on his heel and march back to the wagon. Instead, he forced himself to speak.

14

At his greeting, the thin youth turned to face him. Alton noticed that the boy's lean face was stony with anger and his eyes flashed defiance. Jem took a protective step toward his ma. When Alton recalled the insults the boy had overheard, fresh shame engulfed him, hot and prickly. Alton's lips quivered into what he hoped formed a decently apologetic smile.

Sue Ellen, her back to him, stared straight ahead. From his vantage point Alton saw two tears spill from behind rich, dark lashes to course a wet trail down each curved cheek. Catching the sunlight, the tears glistened like jewels.

Suddenly remembering manners long forgotten, Alton jerked the battered hat from his dark, unruly hair and cleared his throat again to buy time in which to organize his chaotic thoughts.

"Uh, ma'am, where'd it be you folks call home?"

Sue Ellen dabbed a lace hanky to the corner of each eye and swiveled slightly to face him. "S-Salt Creek. I-I don't think it's far. South, somewhere."

"It's your home—'n' you don't know where it's at?" the man blundered, astonished.

"Our *new* home," Sue Ellen corrected mildly, still unwilling to meet his gaze squarely. "But it appears we won't be seeing it anytime soon."

"Hmmm." Alton's dark brows furrowed. When he smiled, it was like sunshine peeking from behind a dark storm cloud. "Why, *I'll* drive you there, ma'am," he offered, feeling expansive and gallant in his effort to undo his recent wrong. "It just so happens I'm goin' right by."

At the news, Sue Ellen lifted her eyes to his, scarcely daring to believe she'd heard correctly. After searching his face, she realized that he was sincere.

15

"How good of you," she breathed with relief. "And where is it you might be heading?"

"Where?" Alton gulped, as her question caught him off guard. "Why. Uh—oh, *south!*" he announced triumphantly, successfully scratching back through the scraps of conversation to recall which direction the widow woman had mentioned. "South!" he repeated cheerfully.

"Then I'm Sue Ellen Stone. Mrs. Nathan Stone." Sue Ellen touched Jem's arm to draw him forward. "And this is my boy, Jeremiah."

"Pleased to meet you—both of you," Alton amended and wrung his felt hat as he ducked his head in greeting.

Jem gave the raven-haired giant a cool look, then extended his hand reluctantly and managed a lukewarm smile.

"Let's get your trunk loaded," Alton suggested to break the stiff silence that lengthened between them.

Together he and Jem wrestled the heavy trunk onto the wagon. But when Jem moved to help his mother, Alton was a step ahead of him. The wagonmaster's large hands encircled Sue Ellen's tiny waist. To his surprise she was light as a milkweed pod as he gingerly deposited her on the seat of the buckboard. With a glance to make sure that the Stones were securely seated, Alton snapped the reins and the team moved forward.

Alton whistled a tuneless song as he drove for several blocks. In that length of time he'd tumbled through his mind the few facts he knew about the Stones, and he felt an uneasy sense of concern.

The woman and her son had only one trunk and a carpetbag between them. It was obvious they weren't taking many possessions to their new home. From the woman's lilting accent, which he couldn't quite place, he suspected they'd traveled a distance to settle in the area.

The trunk, at best, could contain only clothing, linens, maybe some pots and pans, a lamp or two, and a few other odds and ends necessary to set up housekeeping. He was positive they possessed no tools, nothing with which to till the stubborn earth.

"Lady—Miz Stone, I mean—I wonder, have you 'n' your son got any idea what you'll be up agin? Workin' a strange place with no one to help?" Alton asked, reining in the team as they pulled in under the shade of an elm. The impudence in his voice was replaced with concern.

Sue Ellen lifted her chin. "I know it won't be easy," she admitted quietly, "but Jem and I will make it, God willing."

Unconvinced, Alton rubbed his beard. "Maybe you should sell out your land to the first feller who'll give you a decent price. You could settle right here in town." The man spat a stream of brown tobacco juice toward the gutter, then faced Sue Ellen again. "It's safe in town. There's folks close by. And there's always a way for a woman to make a livin', you know." He paused. "There's services people are willin' to pay for."

When Sue Ellen's face flamed scarlet, Alton recognized her humiliation and knew that she'd misunderstood his meaning.

He studied the treetops intently. "Uh—it might be this town would be needin' a librarian," he stammered. "A schoolmarm," he plunged on, desperate to explain, "or a seamstress. I expect you could hire on as a cook, or household help, and have a home for you 'n' your boy by this time tomorrow."

Sue Ellen breathed a soft sigh but made no comment. Alton, deciding that further conversation was dangerous, ripped a plug of tobacco from the chunk in his pouch, folded it, and chucked it into his cheek. With this excuse for silence, he chewed for a few moments before speaking again.

"Ma'am, have you got any money?"

Sue Ellen shot him a look of puzzlement. "Of course. I told you that we plan to *hire* a wagon!"

Once more Alton understood that what he meant did not jibe with what the widow perceived him to be saying.

"That ain't what I was drivin' at!" Alton said in a voice that was almost testy. "The fact is you need money to get started out there on your farm. You don't expect to find sugar in the bowl and flour in the bin, now, do ya? And tools! You've got to have somethin' for the boy to work with."

Sue Ellen frowned. "I have money, yes," she replied. "But I-I didn't stop to think there might not be a town and store close by."

Alton nodded brusquely. "Then you'd better *start* thinkin', ma'am," he suggested, not unkindly. "You can stock up at the general store here in Effingham." He turned the team around.

A few blocks later, Alton halted the horses in front of a large, rambling building. "Don't take long," he ordered. "You'll be wantin' to get to your place by nightfall."

Alton wound the reins in place on the wagon and hopped down. Jem was on the ground before Alton could turn back to assist Sue Ellen.

"I reckon you can find whatever you need here," Alton said.

"I'm sure I can," she agreed.

Sue Ellen smoothed her hair into place and shyly smiled at some of the women she passed on the walk. Their expressions were frankly curious, but their smiles were warm.

With Jem and Alton at her heels, she climbed the steps and entered the cool dimness of the general store.

The floorboards, worn smooth from years of use, creaked softly to announce their presence. A bespectacled clerk gave the three a chipper greeting and poised his pencil in readiness for Sue Ellen's order.

The clerk, who wore a green eyeshade, was alone in the

store. A variety of chairs and crates were pulled up around a cast iron, pot-bellied stove, now cool to the touch. A soft layer of dust coated the flat surface where a coffeepot rested in the winter.

Sue Ellen's eyes swept the store shelves to help her recall what she would need. With long-handled pinchers, the clerk brought down the items she selected. He measured out sugar, flour, coffee, and staples, bundling them neatly.

"Will that be all?" the clerk asked and eyed Sue Ellen over the rim of his glasses that slid down over his thin, pointed nose.

Sue Ellen hesitated a moment, glancing around her once more. "I believe so, thank you."

"I don't think so," Alton said in a flat tone. The clerk glanced from Sue Ellen, to Alton, then back.

Alton faced the widow. "Excuse me, Miz Stone, but you're goin' to a backwoods, dirt-scrabble farm. Once I drop you 'n' the boy off, it won't be easy for you to get back to town. You might not have no close neighbors. So you'd better stock plenty of vittles. And get the young'un tools so's you can make your own way off the land."

"You're right," Sue Ellen sighed, resigned. "I'm afraid I wasn't thinking." Her green eyes surveyed the items stacked in piles in the cavernous room. Alton sensed that she scarcely knew where to begin.

"I can help you pick out the other things you'll need," he offered.

"I'd be ever so grateful if you would."

"You go browse, Miz Stone," Alton suggested. "Your young'un and I can look over the tools 'n' such."

Alton strode to the portion of the store devoted to hardware and implements. Jem tagged along. As Alton explained the various features of axes, shovels, hoes, and small tools, the boy listened intently.

Realizing that she had a precious moment to herself, Sue Ellen wandered through an area that displayed buttons, spools of thread, bolts of fine fabrics, and rolls of ribbon and lace. Though she had allowed her mind to wander, her attention was drawn back to the wooden counter each time a solid *thunk* announced yet another needed purchase. She swallowed hard when she considered the total and thought of the few greenbacks and small coins contained in her worn leather snap purse.

As she idly fingered the ribbons, Sue Ellen turned at Alton's approach and met him with inquiring eyes of the exact shade of the delicate ribbon she held in her hand.

"Uh—," he coughed, embarrassed at the vulnerable look she cast him. "I'd like for you to consider buyin' a canvas tarp."

"A tarpaulin?" She frowned. "I don't understand."

"Just in case that farm of yours ain't got a cabin."

Pure fright glazed Sue Ellen's eyes. Until that moment she hadn't even considered the prospect that there might not be a roof over their heads.

"Oh, yes," she agreed faintly, closing her eyes and drawing on an inner wellspring of strength. "By all means, pick out a tarp."

As Alton strode away to make the selection, Sue Ellen stared blindly at the roll of ribbon clutched in her trembling hands. Her few hair ribbons were faded, the ends fraying and crinkly with permanent wrinkles from being tied and retied.

Another *clunk* sounded from the front of the store. Sighing, Sue Ellen replaced the ribbon on the rack and went to stand beside the counter so as not to be further tempted by the frivolous items displayed.

"That's it," Alton said quietly as he deposited a hammer and pound of nails beside the ax and other tools.

The clerk nodded and began ciphering. When he produced the total, Sue Ellen gave the man a faint smile and reached into her handbag for the snap purse. She unfolded and carefully counted out the greenbacks, then laid one of her precious gold coins beside it, along with enough silver and copper to make exact change.

"A pleasure doing business with you, Mrs. Stone," the clerk said. "We certainly look forward to seeing you next time you folks are in town."

Alton and Jeremiah made several trips to the wagon before Sue Ellen gave the finery one last look of gentle longing and followed them. Alton helped her into the wagon and climbed up beside her. Unwrapping the reins, he clucked to the horses, then groaned, snapping his fingers in disgust as he quickly jerked the reins into a loop around the brake handle and threw down the whip.

"Fergot something I need," he mumbled. "You folks wait right here," Alton ordered, although neither Sue Ellen nor Jem showed any inclination to follow him into the store. "I won't take but a minute."

Idly Sue Ellen looked up and down Jefferson Avenue, admiring the tall buildings that contained a variety of shops to serve the community. She looked back into the general store in time to catch a glimpse of Alton through the window as he strode purposefully toward the counter.

A moment later he emerged, his face strangely flushed. His eyes were alert and darting as he seemed to avoid her gaze and nimbly negotiated the steps from the building, landing on the wagon seat with a bound.

"H—had to get some tobaccy," he announced and tucked a wad in his cheek, conscientiously avoiding Sue Ellen's level

21

gaze. Alton unwrapped the reins, cracked the whip, and started the horses off at a brisk pace.

Feeling like a foolish schoolboy, afraid that Sue Ellen had witnessed his action through the front window, he blushed at the thought. His cheeks burned at the idea of her laughing at him, maybe not so's others could see, but inside, where it'd be even more mocking. He glanced at her. But her serene face seemed proof to him that his secret was safe.

"My, my, but it sure is a hot one today, ain't it?" he asked, hoping to excuse his red face. "Makes me feel as if my face is plumb burnin' up with a fever. I expect I look like a boiled crawdaddy! Sure do hope a breeze blows up soon."

chapter

2

THE DAY WAS unusually warm for late spring, made even more uncomfortable by the hot wind that blew over the land, parching everything in its path.

Alton guided the team down Fourth Street and back over the Pennsylvania Railroad tracks to the south section of Effingham. Sue Ellen marveled at the modern brick homes—three stories tall—some of them almost completely encircled by wide welcoming verandas and sheltered by majestic trees.

Here and there an occasional housewife or hired girl, seeking a moment's rest, waved to the passing wagon from a swing on a shaded porch.

"Isn't this a lovely town?" Sue Ellen asked Jem, who was sitting to her right. He nodded in silent appreciation.

Suddenly aware of the tall stranger at her left, Sue Ellen held herself rigidly upright, careful not to bump against him. As a paying passenger, Sue Ellen didn't know if she were expected to converse with the hired driver or leave him in peace to perform his task.

The wagon creaked and bucked over the rough streets. The bouncing intensified as the brick streets gave way to a rural road of packed clay. To prevent being pitched against the wagonmaster, Sue Ellen clutched the edge of the brightly painted wagon seat until her knuckles turned white.

"How'd you come to settle in Illinois, that is, if you don't mind my askin', Miz Stone?"

Sue Ellen realized that the large man beside her seemed eager for conversation and was not seeking an opportunity to become too familiar. She might have been afraid of him after their rude introduction, but when his concern for her safety surfaced, she sensed he truly wished her no ill.

In fact, Sue Ellen viewed Alton Wheeler as an answer to prayer. She had faith that the Lord had again provided. Crude as he was, Alton Wheeler had been sent to take her to her new home, complete with everything she would need to set up housekeeping.

"We had to settle somewhere," Sue Ellen replied in answer to his question. "My husband, Nat, died of consumption last December. We lived in a company house in the iron mining camp. The boss kindly let us remain until we could make other arrangements."

"I see." Alton nodded.

"Winters in Minnesota are hard, especially on the Mesabi Iron Range near Lake Superior. We had no choice but to stay in Hibbing and do the best we could until it was warm enough to travel. In the meantime, we sold what belongings we couldn't bring with us."

"This farm—it's been in your family?"

"Oh, no," Sue Ellen shook her head. "It belonged to a fellow who worked in the pit with my husband. Nathan loaned him some money. When he couldn't repay, he deeded his farm to my husband. If we hadn't found the deed in Nat's possessions, I truly don't know what would've become of us. A mining town's no place for a woman alone. And we have no relatives to take us in."

His curiosity satisfied, Alton changed the subject.

"Sure is hot," he muttered, mopping his brow with a red handkerchief. "Feels kind of like tornado weather."

Sue Ellen tensed at the word. "You have tornadoes here?"

"'Most every spring. Twisters roar through often enough it gets so you don't pay 'em much mind. No sense worryin' about what you can't change, ma'am."

For the past hour Sue Ellen had been fighting a losing battle with weariness. Eventually her eyes grew heavy and the lids fell shut. Her head bobbed in the warm sunlight, then drooped forward. The bouncing wagon jostled her until Sue Ellen's head came to rest against Alton's solid arm. Tenderly he smiled down at her. He nodded at Jem to move over on the seat to better brace the sleeping woman between them.

"Your poor mama is plumb tuckered out," Alton said softly.

"It's been a long, hard trip."

Alton narrowed his eyes and studied the scrawny youth.

"Son," he said in a hoarse whisper, "have you got any idea what your mama plans to do with that farm?"

Jem shrugged. "Not really."

"I take it you all don't come from a farmin' family?"

"No, sir."

Alton groaned softly and spat into the prairie grass that swayed alongside the trail. "That's what I was afraid of," he muttered, then fell into such intense silence that Jem dared not speak.

Eventually Jeremiah's head sagged forward, and he, too, slept.

Alton slowed the horses' gait and drove at a steady pace, casting an occasional worried eye at the gathering clouds. He knew that the woman and her son needed rest. And chances were the storm would pass them by. He hoped it would.

25

But eight miles south of Effingham, Alton knew that the brewing storm was going to strike. And when it hit, it would hit hard.

There was now a marked chill in the air. The sky grew heavy and swollen with dark, inky clouds that piled together in the southwest. The sun shining against the storm clouds gave them the hue of an angry, purple bruise.

When Jem shifted in his sleep, Alton reached across Sue Ellen's limp form and poked him awake. The boy looked at him questioningly.

"Where'd your mama put that map, boy? I think we're nearin' the place to ford Salt Creek."

Alton's whisper aroused Sue Ellen. Embarrassed, she jerked back from the solid warmth of his arm and reached into her handbag to produce the yellowed paper.

Sue Ellen patted her hair into place, straightened her long skirt, then peered about. Her lips parted in horror when she saw the leaden black clouds boiling across the sky.

"Oh, my goodness!"

"Just a little summer squall." Alton sloughed it off with a casual air. But when he smartly snapped the reins across the horses' backs to quicken their pace, Sue Ellen suspected the truth.

"There's a bad storm coming, isn't there?" she asked, her lips trembling.

"Yes'm, there sure is," Alton admitted. He shouted, and the team broke into a dead run. Sue Ellen knew then just how awful Alton expected the storm to be.

Dark clouds raced toward them, tumbling over each other in their hurry. Lightning forked the sky, and birds in flight darted and hung as if suspended, flapping ineffectively against the stiff wind before surrendering to the air currents and allowing themselves to be borne to the nearest shelter.

The horses, now wild-eyed with fright, thundered over the trail, sending the wagon swerving and bumping over ruts. After poorly negotiating one sharp curve, a wheel tilted into the air, only to land so heavily an instant later that the entire wagon shuddered.

Thunder cracked so close that Sue Ellen screamed and ducked instinctively. The harsh wind flattened the prairie grass. Majestic branches of the towering trees tangled and wrestled as they struggled to stand against the buffeting wind.

Then the rain came.

Large icy drops fell with resounding smacks. The wind blew a wall of water toward them, drenching the three as they huddled together.

Slipping, struggling, the Clydesdales whinnied with alarm. Their breath came in loud gasps and their hooves drummed the packed clay that was fast growing slick beneath the swirling water. Alton had no choice but to rein in the team before they stumbled and grew lame.

"Get the tarp out, Jem, before you both catch your death!"

Jem pawed through the goods and unrolled the stiff canvas. The wind tore at the corners, threatening to billow it away. By now, Sue Ellen's cotton dress was pasted to her skin and her hair fell in dark tendrils, wet and clinging against her pale cheeks.

"Hang on!" Alton yelled. "We've got to ford the creek!"

The team nickered and tossed their heads when Alton edged them toward the steep slope that led to the water's edge. They skidded down the embankment. One horse stumbled but quickly regained his footing as the wagon lurched and rocked precariously down the incline, axles protesting, floorboards creaking as they bowed.

The sky grew dark as night, broken only by brilliant flashes of lightning that split the sky in long, jagged spears. Thunder crashed and rumbled without ceasing. Alton strained to see beyond the sheet of driving rain. The scrubby brush lining the creek bent beneath the tormenting wind. The creek rose fast. Muddy water swirled and bubbled over the rocks and deadfalls. Small twigs broke from huge trees and fell into the creek, spinning dizzily downstream.

The horses pranced into the water, heads bobbing. Their legs threw up a spray as the wooden wagon wheels bumped and bucked over the stones and erosions in the creek bed, and the dirty brown water boiled higher.

"Brace yourselves!" Alton cried. "Easy, Doc. Easy, Dan," he crooned to the Clydesdales. They flopped their ears, seeming to acknowledge his voice as they plunged on.

Sue Ellen stared ahead, her eyes glassy. Her shaking lips moved in prayer.

"Don't worry," Alton reassured her between cracks of thunder. "I'll take care of you. We'll be all right."

She gave him a quick, weak smile.

Doc and Dan started up the slippery bank, the brown clay already slick and gray beneath the downpour. The horses dug their hooves in. Soft sucking sounds filled the air as they mounded mud behind their back legs, plowing up the bank, striving to gain inch by precious inch. The bells tinkled unceasingly as the massive animals panted and strained to haul the awkward wagon out of the creek, but the wagon remained at a dangerous angle, mired in the creekbed.

The Clydesdales' bellies heaved. Their nostrils flared. Straining against their collars until the leather creaked and threatened to snap, they whinnied, then sank even deeper into the mud that bogged the wagon.

Unmindful of the woman and boy, Alton bellowed a stream of violent oaths. Water swirled higher. The swift

28

current tugged at the wagon, lifting it, lowering it, threatening to upset it and sweep it away.

"Take the reins!" Alton ordered.

He wrapped them around Sue Ellen's hands before she could protest, then shoved Jem off the seat and into the water on his side of the wagon. A startled Jem bobbed to the surface and found his footing as Alton thrashed into the water.

"Miz Stone!" Alton yelled. Sue Ellen glanced back, her eyes large with fear. "When I holler, you whup the horses, ya hear?" Alton didn't wait for her answer. He turned to Jem. "Grab a spoke, boy, and lift for all you're worth. We've got to get this wagon out of the water before the creek rises more and takes 'er. Ready now—push!" Alton gritted his teeth. His face grew crimson; his eyes fell shut with exertion. "Push!"

Sue Ellen lashed the horses. Doc and Dan threw themselves against their harnesses, fell back, then flung themselves ahead. Their haunches flattened out. They seemed to sink and blend into the very ground, drawing their strength from the earth as they gained an inch. Then another.

Alton clenched his teeth. Sweat poured from his forehead to be washed away in rivulets of rain. The wagon slid ahead, then skidded sideways, gouging out a crater of mud. Suddenly the wagon groaned as it began to tip.

"Push!" The air resonated with the angry sounds of the storm and the man.

Jeremiah levered his spoke and stared in wonder at the burly giant who seemed intent on lifting the wagon bodily from the mire. He watched as Alton braced his rough boots on the stony creek bed and shoved his massive shoulder against the splintery wagon box.

When it streaked ahead, bouncing, lurching, catapulting up the incline, Alton let out a victory whoop, lost his balance, and fell face-first into the foaming stream.

Sue Ellen, hearing his scream, whipped the team harder. On solid footing again, the horses bolted ahead, racing down the rain-slick trail, frosty manes and tails streaming. Sue Ellen froze in horror as the trees flew by and the wagon again threatened to tip over. She raised her hands to cover her face and dropped the reins. Seeing a boulder ahead, outlined in a flash of lightning, she braced herself for the impact, but the team veered sharply and missed the rock. Nevertheless, the action pitched Sue Ellen from the seat, and she saw the ground rising to meet her mere seconds before she landed with a sickening thud. Sue Ellen groaned, then lay still, too wracked with pain to draw breath.

Alton scrambled over the muddy ground, swearing at the team to halt. He dropped to his knees beside Sue Ellen's still form.

"Over here, Jem!" he called.

At the sound of Alton's voice, Sue Ellen's eyes fluttered open. Strong arms lifted her from the muddy earth. Then she remembered. She tried to speak—but words would not come. Alton's face bent near, his blue eyes darkening to slate.

"Miz Stone! Miz Stone!" Alton shook her gingerly. "Answer me! Please answer me."

"I'm all right," she murmured.

"You're sure? Ain't nothin' broke?"

"I don't think so. I'll be . . . fine—" She ran her hand over her bruised ribs, wincing in pain.

"You scared the starch out of your boy 'n' me. Why on earth did you do a fool thing like whup the team after we'd already cleared the mire?" Alton didn't listen for her response but strode for the wagon, Sue Ellen a damp bundle in his arms.

"Fix your mama a place, Jem."

Jem sprang into action to prepare a makeshift pallet. Then

30

Alton laid Sue Ellen on the floor of the wagon. Pulling dry matches from the tin container in his pocket, he lit his battered kerosene lantern. When Sue Ellen opened her eyes, Alton studied her face. With clumsy fingers he gently removed the muddy, tangled ribbon from her matted hair.

"It's ruined . . . ruined," she sighed. "And it was the only ribbon I had left." Her eyes slipped shut and her head crooked to rest on her shoulder.

Alton touched his pocket to reassure himself that the leather tobacco pouch was there. Though the leather was sopped, maybe the contents were protected by the lining.

"Don't fret none about your hair ribbon," he soothed. "Just be thankful you weren't hurt, or, worse—kilt."

Alton's words trailed off. Tucking a comforter snug beneath Sue Ellen's chin, he walked to the front of the wagon.

Strange new emotions surged through his veins, as intense as the storm that raged around them, as mysterious as nature itself. For the first time he knew what it was to have someone turn to him, trust him, seek his protection, as the woman with the gentle green eyes had done that day, and he felt a pleasant fulfillment unlike any he'd experienced before.

"The storm's passin'," Alton said and joined Jem, taking the wet reins. "Once the clouds clear, it won't be so dark. There's plenty of light yet to make it to the farm. Accordin' to the map, we can't be far."

The horses slogged along the wet path, trailing across the flat Salt Creek bottomland that marked the bed of a prehistoric stream reduced to a mere trickle except during downpours. They struggled along the steep rise to the upland where the path was better marked. A flicker of hope ignited in Alton's heart. Apparently Sue Ellen *would* have neighbors.

"For your mama's sake, boy," Alton spoke, "I hope there's somethin' on that farm of yours."

Grimly Jem nodded. Alton suspected that Jeremiah, like his mother, hadn't considered they might find nothing more than a patch of desolate, unbroken sod.

Sue Ellen eased her way up from beneath the tarp Alton had tucked around her. Realizing that they were nearing the Stones' property, he deliberately avoided her gaze, unwilling to witness the despair in the woman's eyes if it turned out to be a disappointment. Instead, jaw clenched tightly, he concentrated on the horses' broad backs.

Alton didn't know what to expect—but he knew what he feared. Already he had decided that he simply couldn't leave the widow and her son to an uncertain future. Couldn't just deposit them in the wilderness, and abandon the helpless woman, forcing her to fend for her young as best she could.

Beyond a thicket of brush, a faint trail disappeared into the woods. Zig-zagging alongside it was a rickety, weather-beaten, split-rail fence. The lane was untrod; the prairie grass, matted. Alton forced himself to look when Sue Ellen cried out.

"There it is, Jem! We're home! Home at last!"

Sue Ellen struggled from beneath the weight of the tarp. Her eyes shone with happiness, while a slow grin spread across Alton's face.

"Well, well, it 'pears you folks are in luck."

Alton surveyed the area as the horses broke through the tangled underbrush along the trail. In a small clearing on the top of a knobby hill was a snug log cabin sheltered by the spreading branches of massive oak and soft maple trees. A short distance from the cabin in one corner of a cleared pasture stood a barn. Alton laughed with relief, then blinked to make sure it wasn't a vision that would suddenly disappear the next time he looked.

Alton halted the team near the cabin. Seeing her new home, Sue Ellen's eyes misted.

"Isn't it wonderful?" she whispered as he helped her down. "How can I ever thank you for bringing us home? Oh, Jem, *home!*"

The way she spoke the word, Alton knew that it was sweet to her tongue.

"Yup," he agreed. "Home, Miz Stone. And a fine one it looks to be. Must say, I never dared hope you'd find it this good."

"I knew we'd have a home here—or make our own," Sue Ellen said quietly. "God's been good to us, Mr. Wheeler. This is the answer to our prayers—not a case of happenstance. I knew that the Lord wouldn't lead us to a new home and not take care of our needs. We trusted—He provided."

Without another word, Sue Ellen moved on to inspect her surroundings, while Alton stared after her, shaking his head. Then he turned to make his own survey.

Split-rail fences enclosed the area. With only occasional missing slats, Alton knew it wouldn't take over a good day's work to have it in decent repair.

A small shed stood behind the cabin. The stonework led Alton to believe that, beneath the shed, was a root cellar. And the vent convinced him that the building could also be used for smoking and curing meats.

The cabin, solid and squarely built, with the logs tightly chinked, appeared snug enough to endure the worst weather.

"There's enough daylight left to unload the wagon and get you folks settled in if we hurry," Alton said.

Jem helped the big man with the ponderous trunk, while Sue Ellen carried the lantern and led the way. Then Alton motioned to the boy to set down the trunk, and he took the lantern from Sue Ellen.

"You'd best let me check the cabin out before you go in—jest in case varmints have set up housekeepin'."

Not knowing what faced him, Alton swung open the door, the unused hinges whining. Alton held the lantern aloft, and the glow found the walls.

The kitchen was bare save for a large iron cookstove with a warming oven and water reservoir. In the corner a dented copper wash boiler lay on its side, covered with dust and filled with mice ravelings of weeds and grass. A sauerkraut cutter with a broken, rusty blade leaned against one wall.

A rush of scurrying feet offered proof that small creatures indeed inhabited the lonely cabin. Aside from that, there was silence.

Sue Ellen and Jem waited outside on the wide stone that served as a step into the cabin, a pace and a half from the pump in the cistern. They followed Alton's progress by the heavy thud of his footfalls through the cabin. After climbing the ladder to the loft to check for black snakes coiled among the rafters, he returned to pronounce the dwelling safe.

"Everything's fine. Jest fine," Alton assured them. "Nice cabin you've got, Miz Stone. A few inherited pieces of furniture, too. Not much, mind you, but a heap better'n nothin'."

"How wonderful!" Sue Ellen's green eyes shone in the reflected lamplight.

"Now let's get your things out of the weather."

The three filed back to the wagon, then returned to the cabin with armloads of supplies. Jem and Alton stored the tools in the shed while Sue Ellen dug out the lamps packed in the trunk, filled them with oil from the general store, and touched a match to the wicks, quickly bringing warmth and light to her new house.

When she placed a lamp high on a shelf attached to a wall

in the kitchen, it cast a cheerful glow over the entire room. Hesitantly, with Alton's lantern swinging at her side, she made her way through the house, inspecting the main room off the kitchen that led to a bedroom. She wrinkled her nose with distaste at the dust, cobwebs, and dirt.

"Now that we've got everythin' brung up from the wagon," Alton said, stepping in with the last load, "y'all can get right to work."

"Yes . . . and thanks," Sue Ellen said in a distracted tone as he exited the cabin.

Jeremiah's snigger drew her attention.

"And just what do you find so amusing, young man?" she inquired, purposely keeping her voice low.

"*Him*," Jem gestured toward the door. "*Brung!* What kind of grammar is that? His ma didn't do a very good job of teaching him, did she?"

Sue Ellen quelled Jem with a glance. "Perhaps better than I've managed to do with *you!* Better poor speech and a fine heart than fine speech and a poor attitude."

"I'm sorry, Ma." Jem was instantly contrite. "You're right. It's just that he's so . . . different."

"Different, maybe. But no better and no worse than any other man created in God's image."

Grabbing the brand-new bucket that the wagonmaster had insisted she buy, Sue Ellen scurried to the cistern, slammed and clanged the handle, and was rewarded a few seconds later when the leathers coughed up a gushing flow of water. Unmindful of the water that sloshed into her slippers, she rushed into the kitchen, attacking the grime.

She was scarcely aware of the time that had passed until she looked out to discover that it was pitch dark! Alton and Jem leaned in the doorway, watching her work—Alton, with a strange, bemused look on his handsome face; Jem, with the glaze of fatigue dulling his eyes. Her own stomach rumbled.

"Oh, my goodness! I've been so caught up in what I was doing that I completely lost track of the time." Sue Ellen set down the bucket and wiped her hands on her apron. "You both must be starved!" Alton made no answer. Jem shrugged. "Thank the Lord for dry kindling!" Sue Ellen continued, bustling about contritely. She retrieved twigs, snapping them as she crossed to the iron stove. "I'll have a fire going in no time."

"Here. Let me do it," Alton offered.

With a smile, Sue Ellen relinquished the kindling. Alton squatted in front of the firebox of the stove, arranged the firewood just so on the grate, then touched a match to it. Expertly he fed the fire until it was perfect for cooking.

"Supper won't be fancy, Mr. Wheeler, but I promise you it'll be filling. My, won't a cup of hot coffee taste good after what we've been through today?"

Alton nodded. "But don't go to no trouble on my account."

Sue Ellen looked up from the crockery bowl where she was fingering together flour, lard, and leavening. "I won't fuss. Can't." She gave a soft laugh. "Tonight will be plain fare. But I promise better, come morning."

From the coffeepot, now perking cheerily, came the rich aroma of the delicious brew. Beside it, on the cookstove, Sue Ellen placed a seasoned cast-iron skillet, where a snowy mound of lard was soon sizzling and sliding across the surface.

Deftly she formed the dough into patties and dropped the biscuits into the hot grease. When she wiped her hand across her face, she left a smidgen of flour on the tip of her nose.

Suddenly her eyes were drawn to Alton's and she flushed, startled by the intensity of his gaze.

Feeling shaken himself, Alton forced his eyes away. He didn't dare look at her again, for fear she could see written plainly on his face the strange and wonderful sensations he was feeling.

For, standing in a grimy kitchen, her dress damp from rain, an apron tied around her waist, her hair spilling from its neat coronet, and a dollop of flour dotting her pert nose, Sue Ellen Stone was the most beautiful and appealing woman Alton had ever seen in his life!

A sardonic smile twisted his lips. How odd. The barroom girls at the Idle Hour with their scented, powdered flesh, their artfully styled hair, their fawning, simpering manner had never aroused in him the emotions that Sue Ellen had just now.

Suddenly Alton was bitterly aware of how many of life's priceless treasures he had missed while searching for excitement. Small, homey things. Simple pleasures. Joy in unexpected places. And until now, he had not known he was missing them. Embarrassed by his own thoughts, he cleared his throat.

Sue Ellen spread a cross-stitched tablecloth over the trunk to form a makeshift table. The two men perched on blocks of aged firewood that had been stacked in the corner of the kitchen behind the stove while she served the biscuits and black coffee.

Alton reached for a biscuit but jerked his hand back and peeked at Sue Ellen and Jem, who seemed to be waiting for something. Sue Ellen bowed her head. Jem followed suit. Alton lowered his head a fraction of an inch, then regarded the Stones from the corner of his eye while Sue Ellen solemnly asked the Lord's blessing.

Throughout the simple meal she chattered about her plans for transforming the cabin into a real home.

"It'll be downright cozy when you're done, Miz Stone."

"Jem can do something about the long grass. And the shrubs. The roses will need to be pruned so they'll bloom better. That lilac bush needs trimming back, too." She sipped her coffee. "We'll make out fine. Don't worry about us when you go, Mr. Wheeler. The Lord's watched out for us so far. We're trusting Him to continue. We're thankful for all you've done for us, of course, going out of your way on our account, but we don't want to delay you any longer."

"'Twern't nothin'," Alton said modestly.

"Well, even so, it's been much appreciated and we don't want to hinder you further. I know you need to be on your way."

"Yes, ma'am," he said quietly.

To Alton, Sue Ellen's words sounded for all the world like a dismissal. And suddenly he knew just how much he wanted to stay—at least for a few days so he could help the boy learn to master the tools. Teach Jem the things he'd need to learn to be ready for winter. Satisfy himself that the widow and her son were settled in and acquainted with neighbors who could come to their aid in time of trouble.

"I'll bed down in the barn with my horses tonight, if you don't mind, Miz Stone. Then we can leave at first light."

"Whatever you say, Mr. Wheeler," Sue Ellen agreed.

For a brief instant Alton thought that he detected reluctance in Sue Ellen's eyes. *Reluctance that he was staying? Or that he planned to leave? Probably because he was staying,* Alton decided. Widow women had to be careful. Tongues got to wagging soon enough as it was.

"Don't go before Jem and I thank you with a good breakfast, though," Sue Ellen warned when Alton arose. "I wouldn't think of letting you leave hungry after all you've done for us. We'll remember you as our friend, Mr. Wheeler, and mention you often in our prayers."

Alton accepted her words silently. For the life of him, he couldn't think what to say to a woman who set such store by God. He stretched and yawned.

"Well, guess I'll be turnin' in. If somethin' happens in the night—you just holler. I sleep light. I'll come runnin'."

"I'm sure we'll be fine," Sue Ellen said. "Oh, by the way, you'll need cover. Do you have a quilt?"

Alton grunted a vague reply that afforded no direct answer.

"Do you have a dry quilt or not, Alton?" Sue Ellen repeated the question, flushing when she realized that she'd used his given name. "Y-you've been soaked to the skin."

Not bothering to wait for a reply, she dug into the trunk and produced a beautiful new quilt—thick, soft, and colorful. She held it out to Alton, but he tried to refuse.

"Take it," she insisted.

"I can't, ma'am. It ain't right to take a quilt like that to a barn."

"Take it and keep it. It's yours. I'm giving it to you. Quilting's one thing I enjoy almost more than anything else. I gave away a passel of quilts before we left. After we get settled here, I'll make more. Take this—with our thanks."

"If you say so," Alton said in a gruff voice and tucked it under his arm with a shy nod. "See you in the mornin' then."

"Good night, Mr. Wheeler."

Alton paused but didn't turn to face her. "I liked it better when you called me Alton," he spoke into the darkness.

"Then good night, . . . Alton."

Only then did he glance back to see her slender figure silhouetted in the doorway. "G'night to you, Miz Stone—uh, Sue Ellen."

Alton trudged toward the team, whistling happily, eyeing storm clouds gathering once more to blot the stars from sight. He was humming under his breath when he unhitched the horses and turned them into the pasture.

Picking up the lantern and quilt from the wagon seat, he noticed a glimmer from something on the ground reflecting the lantern's rays. Alton stooped and held the lantern close. It was a square piece of paper. When he turned it over, his eyes fell on a small, sepia-toned portrait of Sue Ellen Stone!

Alton's heart flew to his throat and disturbed his breathing. Just looking at this woman's likeness brought him joy unlike anything he'd ever known. For a moment he cupped the picture in his large hand and held it against his chest. Then he tucked it into the pocket of his jacket.

Glancing toward the cabin, he knew that the small woman was no doubt busily getting settled in. The dust, cobwebs, and grime were causing her such worry. A smile encased Alton's features. Come morning, he'd be up at daybreak, and he'd make Sue Ellen the finest broom in Effingham County. It would be his going-away present.

Alton hated to roll out the pretty quilt onto the packed dirt floor of the barn, so he scratched together enough dusty straw to form a mat. Then he unfolded the quilt, shucked his damp clothes, and nestled under the soft luxury of Sue Ellen's gift. Wrapped in its folds, he attempted to sink into the sweet pleasure of sleep. Instead, he lay wide awake, reliving the events of the unusual day.

It was hours later when he first heard the horses nickering. The wind had gusted, howling through missing chinks. Now the Clydesdales, having crossed the pasture, stepped under the lean-to attached to the barn, their tails switching rhythmically.

The sky opened with a crack of thunder, followed by a bolt

of lightning that cleaved the heavens. Rain fell in a torrent and swelled to a cascade that poured from the shake-shingle roof.

When Alton finally fell asleep, a smile curved his lips. He wouldn't be leaving come morning, after all. And no busybody could make anything of it!

He had known that the creek was rising fast when they crossed it. Now Little Wabash River would flood and back up the smaller tributaries for miles around. With a real gully-washer like this, Salt Creek could stay flooded for days!

Alton didn't know much about this God that Sue Ellen Stone talked about and prayed to. But he knew that he wanted it to rain and rain. And Alton ventured a heartfelt prayer that it would.

chapter

3

WITH THE BIRDS heralding the morning sun, Alton sat up and shook the sleep from his eyes. Instead of sleeping lightly as he'd promised Sue Ellen, he'd slept like one dead while the storm blew itself out.

And what a storm it had been! If the puddles surrounding the barn were any indication, the creeks would doubtless be a roaring torrent stretching across the vast bottomland.

Hurriedly Alton dressed and jerked his fingers through his thick black hair before stepping into the morning light.

He noticed the stream of smoke curling from the cabin's stone chimney. Sue Ellen must be stirring up the fire to begin the day. When he learned that it would be a while before she'd have their meal ready, he walked to the ridge and surveyed the flooded land. It was just as he expected— flooded from hill to hill!

Doc and Dan approached, pausing to nip tasty morsels of lush grass along the way.

"Take your time, boys," Alton called happily. "We won't be leavin' today." He smacked the rump of the gelding, then caressed the stallion's thick neck.

The horses moseyed off while Alton collected stiff stems of dried prairie grass. Back in the barn, he made Sue Ellen's broom, all the while imagining her response when he presented it to her.

When he suspected that breakfast might be ready, he went to the cabin, clutching the gift behind his back.

"This here's fer you," he said, thrusting the broom into her hands. His face grew crimson, but his gaze didn't waver.

Delight erased the fatigue in Sue Ellen's features.

"Aren't you a dear to think of that!" Her hand flew to her lips when she realized how familiar she sounded. "I, uh, it's very kind of you. The cabin needs a good cleaning," she added stiffly.

Alton accepted Sue Ellen's invitation to be seated at the makeshift table. Then she bustled around serving the food. She moved quickly. Alton assumed that it was so he could be on his way. He cleared his throat to draw her attention.

"Miz Stone—I'm afraid I can't leave this mornin'." Alton plunged ahead before Sue Ellen could speak. "The creek—it's flooded. There's no way to get around it. Bishop Creek'll stop me south of Fiddler's Ridge, too."

Sue Ellen nodded. "It rained with a vengeance most of the night. You're more than welcome to stay in the barn and break bread with us as long as need be. You've been a real friend to us."

"Thanks, ma'am," Alton murmured. "Since I can't leave, I may as well make myself useful. There's plenty of farmin' the boy and I can get started before I have to go."

"There's no call to earn your keep. You've already done that . . . and more."

Alton stared at his folded hands. "Maybe so . . . but I'd like to." He paused and met her eyes. "I hardly know how it'll feel again after all these years."

Sue Ellen busied herself with the breakfast. "You come from a farming family, Mr. Wheeler—Alton?"

"Born on a farm," he replied. "Over in Missouri. But I've been away most of my life. Some things, though, it seems you never forget."

With a few direct questions, Sue Ellen coaxed Alton's story from him. His father had died from blood poisoning when Alton was five years old. The Wheeler family, two sons and a daughter, moved to a small town near St. Louis the following year. Two years later, Alton's mother was dead of influenza. Then the children had gone their way, making their livelihood as best they could. In the ensuing years Alton had lost touch with his brother and sister.

As vague as Alton was about the past, especially the recent years, Sue Ellen sensed he wasn't comfortable speaking of them. Out of respect for his feelings, she changed the subject. When Alton turned the conversation to her life, Sue Ellen answered his questions without evasion.

"The mornin's flyin' by," Alton observed, snapping open the case to consult his gold pocket watch after breakfast. "I believe I'll hitch the team and go callin' on your new neighbors. Care to come along, Jem?" The boy's response was immediate and enthusiastic. Alton turned to Sue Ellen. "How about you, Miz Stone?"

"Sue Ellen," she corrected with a soft, quick smile. "I'd like to go, Alton, but truly, I can't spare the time. Do give my greetings and regrets to the neighbors, though."

Immediately after Alton and Jem left the cabin, Sue Ellen followed suit, pumped the shiny bucket full of water, and turned to do battle with the accumulated dust and dirt of many years.

Alton taught Jem to hitch the horses and allowed him to drive the team. Smiling at Jem's elation, Alton's thoughts wandered elsewhere. He wondered what kind of people the Stones' neighbors would be. What if they were hardhearted people, who would not care a whit if the widow woman and her son lived or died?

The more he thought about it, the more grateful Alton was that Sue Ellen had not chosen to accompany them that morning. For his own peace, if it required a surreptitious exchange of money for neighborly service, then so be it. But he must keep such knowledge from Sue Ellen. It would not do for her to know the neighbors were being paid to call on her. If he came up with enough from the wad in his pocket, perhaps they would even agree to check on the Stones every week.

By the time Jem slowed the team to negotiate the turn into the path leading to the deep woods, Alton had the words framed to broach the business deal. With that solved, he was now scratching for an excuse to send Jem off on a wild-goose chase so the boy wouldn't overhear the plans.

Smoke curling from the chimney confirmed Alton's notion that a family lived in the woods. He looked around, admiring the neat farmstead, noticing similar improvements he hoped to accomplish around Sue Ellen's place before he departed.

The team's tinkling harness bells announced their arrival before Jem or Alton had a chance to hail the tall, sandy-haired farmer who stepped outside the cabin, carrying an ax.

"Halloo!" the man called and sauntered toward them. His gray eyes were openly welcoming.

"Howdy," Alton said stiffly.

The man hesitated. "Somethin' I can do for you folks?"

Alton searched for words. He could hardly speak his piece with Jem still standing beside him.

"Uh . . . just come over to get acquainted." He drew a deep breath. "You folks have got yourself some new neighbors— the Widow Stone and her boy, Jeremiah, here. I hauled them out from Effingham yesterday afternoon. We got caught in the storm. What a toad-strangler that was!"

"Amen to that!" the man agreed. "The ground was dry enough, though, so we could use the rain."

"The creeks are out," Alton said pointedly, "so I couldn't leave today, as I'd planned." He hopped down from the wagon and extended his hand. "The name's Alton Wheeler."

The farmer returned his grip. "William Preston, here," he replied. "Will, to my friends." He leaned the ax against the trunk of a hickory tree. "Come in and say hello to the missus."

"We'd be pleased to," Alton said, entertaining hope that there'd be children, and that he could arrange for a private moment to make his offer to Will Preston while Jem's attention was taken elsewhere.

Will ushered them into the cabin. "Fanchon! We've got company!"

A stout, ginger-haired woman with freckles and snapping brown eyes nodded her head in silent greeting.

"Fanny, this here's Alton Wheeler," Will explained. "He delivered the Widow Stone and her boy to that abandoned farm up the road apiece."

Fanny tucked a stray wisp of hair behind her ear and looked up with a smile. "Pleased to meet you. And I'll be proud to be makin' acquaintance with Miz Stone, too."

"I know she'd feel the same," Alton said, sizing up the woman and deciding she'd do nicely as a friend for Sue Ellen. "Miz Stone asked me to give you her respects and regrets that she couldn't come visitin' today. She's got chores stacked up like cordwood. The cabin's a mess—and it's worryin' her to death."

Fanny chuckled. "Oh, woe 'n' bedraggle, don't I know what that's like? What a time we had before we built this cabin. There was a lean-to, which was better than nothing, but I thought I'd died and gone to heaven when Will and some of the folks finished this cabin and I walked through the door to stay."

After chatting for a few minutes, Will led the way outside, and Fanny returned to the kitchen.

"Fine team you've got there." Will squinted at the Clydes- dales and stepped closer to examine them, stroking their velvety noses. "A pair like that would sure make a fellow's workday easier."

"Prime horseflesh," Alton agreed proudly. "Got 'em from a German farmer over near St. Louis." But he kept to himself the fact that, along with the gold pocket watch and wagon, he'd won them on the turn of a card in a poker game. "They're a good draft breed—workers, those two. Surprisin', but that stallion's as gentle as a kitten!"

"You don't say," Will murmured admiringly. "You're a fortunate man."

Alton was thoughtful. He scratched his beard and stared off into the distance as a fresh idea came to him. Maybe if he did Will Preston a favor, the man would feel beholden to check on the widow and her son.

"If you're in need of borrowin' my team—I'd be happy to oblige. Might be days before Salt Creek goes down enough to allow me passage. You could make good use of the horses until then."

Will hesitated. "Well . . . there are some things my horses haven't the strength and pullin' power to handle," he admitted.

"Then it's settled." Alton closed the deal quickly. "I vow that if you can chain these horses up to it, Doc and Dan can haul it. The horses are yours to use while I'm in these parts."

"I can't take advantage of your generosity," Will said. "You may need those horses yourself some days. Why don't we work out a swap?"

"Suits me fine and dandy!" Alton agreed, now that Jem was out of sight and earshot. "You can use my horses, and, in exchange, you check in on the Widow Stone after I'm gone—'thout lettin' her know that was our agreement, of course."

Will stared, startled.

Alton flushed. "I'll be happy to kick in some jack, too," he murmured, reaching for his wallet.

"That's an unfair deal, man," Will sputtered.

What more could the man want? Alton screwed up his face as if trying to think up more bargaining leverage.

"I meant unfair to *you*, friend, not to me! Why, we'd fully expected to drop in on the widow woman. That's only bein' neighborly. 'Sides, Fanny'd like havin' another woman 'round for quiltin' bees and talkin' things over with 'n' such."

Alton was stunned. In taverns like the Idle Hour, men struck hard bargains and gave no quarter. But before him stood a man who was concerned with exchanging value for value.

"Wh—what would you suggest then?"

"Well, I'll tell you what," the farmer went on. "After you're gone, I'll have only my horses—none of them near as big as these beauties of yours."

"True—"

"I'd like to use a sire like your stallion with my mares. They'll be in soon. Serviced by your stud, the foals could lighten the load in years to come. By then my boy Rory, who's six now, could handle the small team, and I could break in the new team with good draft blood in 'em."

Alton was interested. "Count on me to help out any way I can."

"If you're willin', would you consider two shoats a fair trade? An' a couple bushel of corn to see you through to harvest? They'd put meat on the table for the Stones this winter." Will paused. "There's menfolk in the neighborhood who'd be glad to butcher for the widow woman. Iffen she

49

don't know how to salt, cure, 'n' smoke the meat, Fanchon can teach her handily enough."

"More 'n' fair," Alton was quick to respond. "I'm sure enough satisfied if you are."

"Then it's a deal!" Will said happily.

As Will made plans for the remaining days of the week, Alton listened absently and occasionally grunted what he hoped was an appropriate comment. Inside, his heart was soaring with the knowledge that his fears of the morning were groundless. He had worried himself half-sick trying to figure a way to assure a bit of security for Miz Stone and her boy— even to bribing the neighbors if need be. And look at the fine folks she had living almost within hollering distance?! Folks who gave in full measure, unconcerned with what they received in return.

Sue Ellen's words rose to haunt him. With glowing eyes she had told him that the Lord had always cared for them. That they had trusted Him in the past and they would trust Him with the future to provide as He saw fit, or to show them how to make do with what they had.

Could it be that there was something to this God talk, after all? Alton gave it a moment's thought. But then Alton Wheeler, not some invisible God, had provided for the Stones this time, hadn't he?

He shook his head as if to clear it of the confusion and turned to help Will herd the pigs into an enclosure. They sorted out the sow, who was making uncooperative sounds, and closed the rough gate behind them. Then they set about capturing the pigs, wrestling them into a burlap bag that they set in the wagonbed.

Fanchon, her tiny feet propelling her great bulk forward, rushed from the house with a loaf of fresh sourdough bread wrapped in brown grocer's paper. As she placed it on the wagon seat, Will explained the swap to her, and Fanny beamed her approval.

"Alton, you 'n' Jem wait here just a minute," Fanny ordered. She scurried off and a bit later, wild squawks and whoops could be heard erupting from the henhouse. When Fanny returned, she was carrying a wooden crate filled with yellow straw. An angry bantam hen sat in the box, blinking solemnly, clucking and ruffling her feathers with indignation.

"Take this hen to Miz Stone," Fanny instructed. "She's been settin' a week now. Another two weeks, and she'll have a dozen peeps trailin' her. Later on, Will can catch one of those cocky braggarts and I'll send over a rooster, too."

Alton reached for his pocket. "Sue Ellen will be tickled with the hen. How much do I owe you?"

Fanny's mouth dropped open, her eyes registering shock. "Why, Alton Wheeler, you don't owe me a thing, and I'd be insulted if you tried to pay."

Alton shifted uncomfortably. "Well, I—"

"I understand," she consoled him. "I remember when we were new in these parts. There was an old lady lived on a farm a stretch away. Dead now, she is, God rest her soul. She brought me over a few chickens. I guess she knew how hard it is to set up a farm. Just like you, Alton, I tried to pay her. She laughed in my face, gave me a big hug, and said, 'Someday, honey, pass along the favor to someone else, and consider the debt paid.' So, that's exactly what I'm doin' now—and have done time and time again. If the widow feels beholden to me, you tell her the same thing I was told: 'Pass along the kind favor and consider the debt paid.'"

"That's a right nice thought," Alton said.

Fanny nodded. "Fine way to live. Guess the neighbors around here are so busy payin' each other back that no one ever does without."

"Miz Stone will make you a good neighbor, too," Alton said. "You'll get along. You think a lot alike."

"Hurry back!" Fanny called after them as they were leaving.

"Sure thing," Alton promised with a wave. "I'll be back with the team after dinner, Will."

On the way back to the farm, Alton and Jem discussed a place to keep the shoats and chicken.

"A dab of hard work and we'll have your farm off to a good start. I can't wait to see your mama's face when she sees pigs, a settin' hen, and even some feed corn."

Carrying the warm bread, Alton went to the cabin while Jeremiah unhooked the team. Alton knocked, but got no answer. When he heard thumps inside the house, he decided that Sue Ellen was too busy cleaning to hear his knock, so he entered unbidden.

Sue Ellen was in the sitting room, near the hearth. Her slim shoulders heaved as she knotted her fingers into green and white satiny material and strained to tear it.

"Stop that!" Alton cried.

Startled, Sue Ellen whirled in fright until she saw it was only Alton. Then she began the attempt anew.

Alton was across the room in two steps.

"What in tarnation do you think you're doin' to that dress?"

"Making curtains," Sue Ellen replied crisply and gave another futile yank. "That is, if I can get the silly material to tear, I am."

"Please don't," Alton said softly. He took the silken garment into his hands, where it snagged on the calluses, crackling over his rough skin as he stroked the soft fabric. "'Twould be a pity to ruin such a pretty frock."

"But it's all I've got to make curtains with," she protested.

"The day'll come when you'd regret spoilin' that pretty dress. You'd be better off with nothin' hangin' at your windows."

"Pretty dress—pretty curtains," Sue Ellen said brusquely.

Alton sucked in a deep breath. "It'll never flatter the windows the way it must suit you, Miz Stone."

She took the gown from him, smoothed its lustrous folds, and held it up against her. "It was my best dress—once."

"It will be your best dress again. You won't be wearin' mournin' dresses forever. In your heart I know you must feel like the day will never come when you don't ache for your dead husband. But it will, I'll wager."

Sue Ellen looked shaken.

"I—I—" She looked at the dress, then at the barren window. "I suppose you're right."

"Promise me you won't tear up that dress."

"But what will I do for curtains?" she asked weakly.

Alton shrugged. "You've done without a lot of things. You can do without curtains 'til you get a chance to buy some calico or gingham."

"Ma!" Jem burst into the cabin. "Did Alton tell you 'bout the pigs? And the hen? Come see!"

"Pigs? Chickens?" Sue Ellen gave the two a mystified stare.

Alton sketched in the details. "So, now you've got yourself a start in livestock. It means I'll have to stay on a few more days, maybe even a few weeks, dependin' on Will's horses. So I guess I can't leave when the creek goes down."

"I see—" Sue Ellen breathed.

Mistaking the brevity of her speech for another dismissal, Alton spoke quickly. "I—I expect I can bunk in Will Preston's barn. Or camp alongside my wagon somewhere, if it's an inconvenience havin' me here."

"It's no trouble," Sue Ellen assured him, smiling. "You're welcome to stay on."

The following days found Alton as busy outside the cabin as Sue Ellen was inside. When Alton wasn't fulfilling his end of the bargain with Will, he was using the horses to work the farm. With Will's help and equipment, Alton put in a small patch of corn and plowed a little garden to accept the abundance of plants and seeds Fanny was so willing to share.

Many an evening Alton toyed with the idea of hitching the team to leave at dawn, but before he could leave, the rains again came to clog the stream. When the creek had dwindled enough to allow a wagon to ford, Alton noticed things that must be done before he could leave the widow and her son to face the cold months alone.

In fact, Alton's hands were seldom idle. He felled trees and taught Jem to work the crosscut saw to lop them into stove lengths. He tended the garden and plowed the field. He rechinked a section of the barn.

Eventually he quit mentioning any plans to leave and, with relief, he noticed Sue Ellen no longer spoke of his departure, either.

Evenings, when the weather was fit, Alton hitched up the team and the three called on the Prestons or entertained Fanny, Will, and their children at the Stone farm.

In Fanny Preston, Sue Ellen found a loyal and loving confidante. The plump, older woman was a person of faith as deep as Sue Ellen's, and she welcomed the newcomers with infectious enthusiasm. Will became Alton's trusted friend. And Jem tolerated Fanny's niece who was his own age, and he allowed six-year-old Rory to tag along with him.

"Will and I got word that the pastor will be ridin' through again, Sue," Fanny announced one day when she met their wagon at the gate. "We're hopin' you folks will attend so we can have a good turnout for the gatherin'."

"How wonderful!" Sue Ellen cried. "I've missed worship services these weeks."

"The young pastor gives a fine sermon. He's a quiet man but a nice fellow."

"Then we'll look forward to meeting him."

"Pastor Clark married up my Lizzie to her Harmon the last time he was through," Fanny explained. She dropped her voice to a hushed whisper. "Lizzie's not feelin' too pert these days. She's a slim slip of a girl, so maybe you've noticed she's in the family way. Startin' to look right motherly. Lizzie blushes like fury, though, if one of us remarks about her condition."

Sue Ellen clapped her hands together. "Fanny, how exciting! You'll love having a little one around again. How soon?"

"Let's see, now," Fanny said, ticking off the months on her fingers. "The end of October, Lizzie says."

"I'll be praying for a mild winter so it's easy on the babe."

"We're plannin' a barn raisin' for Lizzie and Harm this summer," Fanny went on. "They'll be needin' plenty of milk, so Will's givin' them a cow."

"You told Sue about the barn raisin'?" Will asked, entering the cabin in time to catch Fanny's words. "I plumb forgot to give Jem and Alton the news."

"Be glad to help out," Alton offered.

Will smiled ruefully and clapped Alton's muscular shoulder. "Well, neighbor, we were kind of countin' on you and your team to hoist the rafters into place. But we wondered if we should ask, for fear you'd put aside your own plans."

"Got nowhere to go, really," Alton admitted. "We'll build your gal and her man a good stout barn." He paused and watched for Sue Ellen's reaction. "Then," he breathed the words, "I'll think hard 'bout leavin'." *Sue Ellen looked disturbed,* he thought, even though she was smiling at Fanny with apparent unconcern.

"I was tellin' Sue that the pastor's ridin' through these parts. She said they'd come to services," Fanny told Will.

"I . . . Jem and I will be there," Sue Ellen corrected. "If the church is in walking distance, that is, or if we have a way."

"It's not far," Will said. "You're more than welcome to ride with us."

"I'll take her 'n' the boy." Alton's quiet, decisive voice ended further discussion.

Fanny's brown eyes sparkled. "I was hopin' you'd say you would, Alton Wheeler. You're a good man, you rascal," she said and shook a teasing finger at him. "Not that you couldn't be better! So could we all, for that!" She chuckled, setting her dimples to dancing.

Will winked at Alton. "All the neighbors make a day of it," he explained. "Some come quite a distance, so we have a basket social when the weather's nice."

"It'll give you folks the chance to meet some of the neighbors, too," Fanny added. "All of them are good folks. They're sure to cotton to you all."

That night on the drive home, Alton talked of the barn raising while Sue Ellen pondered the upcoming worship services.

The next day Will Preston came by to mention that he planned to make a trip to nearby Watson, a small town south and west of Effingham. Its few stores offered some of the necessities and saved the longer drive to the county seat.

"Is there anything you want me to pick up for you, Sue, when I go in to get the goods on Fanchon's list?"

Will's offer was like a dream come true. "Oh my, yes!" she replied brightly. Quickly Sue Ellen wrote out her list on a scrap of brown grocery paper. She knew that with the right ingredients—unusual items she couldn't keep on hand—her pies, cake, and covered dishes would be second to none at the Sunday picnic.

On Saturday Sue Ellen scrubbed their best clothes so they'd

be fresh and clean on Sunday morning, then created a whirlwind in the kitchen, bustling around to fix the food to take along.

Alton shined up the harness, swept the wagon, and groomed Doc and Dan until they glistened, even plaiting their manes so they rippled in waves when he loosened the braids.

Jem slicked his hair back a dozen times in hopes his unruly cowlick would be tamed by morning.

Sunday dawned clear, bright, and warm.

"Nice day, ain't it?" Alton asked when he arrived at the cabin for breakfast.

"Glorious!" Sue Ellen agreed. "Just glorious. The Lord's provided us with perfect weather for gathering together on His day."

After breakfast, Sue Ellen changed into a dress of sturdy black cotton fabric. She checked her hair, tucking stray tendrils into place, then draped a crisp, white starched linen cloth over the wicker basket of food.

By the time they were packed and on the road, several other wagons rumbled along the trail leading to the church on the bluff. Once, Alton halted to let a team on the main path go by. The stranger nodded his thanks, and the bonneted woman beside him wiggled her fingers at Sue Ellen and flashed her a merry grin. The children, sitting stiff and proper so they wouldn't soil their Sunday clothes, eyed Jem as openly as he regarded them.

Sue Ellen sighed with happiness and hugged her Bible to her.

"Lots of folks here," Alton observed as he pulled into the churchyard. "Looks like the whole neighborhood's turnin' out."

Teams were tethered everywhere. Alton halted his horses in

a small clearing, then stepped down to help Sue Ellen from the wagon before he bounded back to the spring seat.

Puzzled, Sue Ellen studied him. "Alton, what's wrong? I—I thought you were going with us."

Alton looked surprised. "Not me, ma'am. No sirree!"

"B—but you said you'd—take me to church. Jem and me. That night over at Fanny's—" Her eyes moistened with disappointment.

"That's right. I said I'd *take* you. But I didn't say I'd go in, did I?"

Sue Ellen thought back to their conversation and swallowed hard as the bitter disappointment settled like a dry lump in her throat.

"No, you didn't at that," she admitted. "But, Alton, Jem and I'd be happy and proud to have you sit with us. Won't you? Please?"

Alton stared at the rough boards of the wagon floor beneath his feet. He realized that Sue Ellen had never asked him for anything before. Never begged. He'd always gotten pleasure in knowing her mind, somehow, and doing little things before she could think to ask. Alton considered her request for a long moment before sagging back into the wagon seat.

"No." His answer was resolute, flat, definite.

"But why not?" Sue Ellen blurted. The question hung in the still air.

"For one thing—my clothes ain't good enough."

Sue Ellen almost giggled in relief. "Alton Wheeler, I'm surprised at you! Why, the Lord doesn't care about your clothes. He cares about *you*. He wants you with Him."

Alton didn't move even as he sensed Sue Ellen's hopeful eyes on him. He knew his refusal would hurt her further, but he felt he had no choice. He couldn't remember the last time he'd been inside a church, but it had been years ago, when he was still a tot at his mama's side.

He didn't know exactly what people did inside churches, but he knew it wasn't for him. Much as part of him wanted to be seated beside Jem and Sue Ellen—like family—another part of him refused to shame the two people he'd come to love by doing the wrong things. Or, worse still, doing the things that might be expected of him.

"You go on in," Alton urged. "I'll wait right here. Religion—well, it's all right for you womenfolk, youngsters, and some fancy Dans and weak sisters. But I've never had any need for it before," he said gruffly, "and I don't expect to start now."

"Very well," Sue Ellen said quietly. She forced a smile, but part of her heart seemed to break right off, leaving her hollow and aching with emptiness. "We all need the Lord, Alton. He wants each one of us. But that's not enough. We've got to want Him, too." Her green eyes clouded with pain as she turned to enter the little building.

Outside, Alton sat and swatted the flies that buzzed around his face. Horses nickered and swished their tails, flicking the pesky insects from sensitive hides. A blue jay cried raucously from a nearby shade tree.

Through the open window of the church house, Alton caught occasional murmured responses—reverent and restrained. And when the congregation blended their voices in song, he was surprised to find that some of the tunes were vaguely familiar.

Alton stirred uncomfortably and was relieved when the people began to drift from the church in congenial clusters. Jumping from the wagon seat, he was at last glad to make himself useful again and hurried to carry the lunch basket to the shady spot beneath a sycamore tree where Sue Ellen had spread their blanket next to Fanny and Will's.

A wagon bed, which served as the community serving table, soon held the dishes and delicacies prepared by the womenfolk. Leaving Sue Ellen and Fanny to spread the contents of their hampers, Alton and Will sauntered over to join the group of men who were discussing the progress of their crops and the likelihood of an early harvest. Jem had long since found some friends his own age and was thrashing about in the trickle of creek that adjoined the church grounds.

The afternoon passed pleasantly, with appetites more than satisfied and conversation beginning to ebb as the men dozed under the shade trees and the women rinsed the dirty dishes in the creek. Here and there, the smallest children rubbed their eyes and toddled over to climb onto their mothers' laps. And even the older boys and girls were content to sit and talk quietly, lulled to lethargy by the abundant food and warm afternoon breezes.

So Sue Ellen was not prepared, when she looked over at Alton, to find a frown shrouding his features. And even when he forced a smile, it failed to reach his troubled eyes. She was glad when he suggested they leave early. Gladder still when Will and Fanny Preston dropped by on their way home to talk over the events of the day.

No sooner had the men left to go look at the cornfield than Fanny bent close to Sue Ellen. "That Alton—isn't he something?" she chuckled.

"What do you mean?" Sue Ellen asked hesitantly.

Fanny made a face and airily waved her plump hand. "Surely you noticed! He's been a grump all afternoon!"

"I *had* noticed," Sue Ellen admitted reluctantly. "But I was hoping that others hadn't. Fanny, I can't for the life of me figure out what's gotten into that man."

"Then you're the only one who doesn't know, Sue."

"Know what?"

Fanny grinned. "That Alton Wheeler is positively sick with jealousy!"

"Jealous?! Of who? And why?"

"Of some of the handsome fellas you were introduced to. That young widower—the farmer—from over toward Eberle, for one. He was impressed with you, Sue. Alton could tell it. Unless I miss my guess, that fella'd like to come courtin' someday. Alton probably sensed that, too. Right then's when his attitude changed, I noticed. That likeable polecat *glared* at every man who looked to have a notion to come over and make your acquaintance."

"Fanny!"

"It's true," Fanny defended stoutly. "I witnessed it with my own eyes. You're a right pretty woman, Sue. Just because you're a widow don't mean the men aren't noticin' that you're pleasin' to the eye.

"Nathan Stone was a lucky man. I don't doubt other men—like Alton—view you as ideal wife material, too. Why, even my Will remarked about what a handsome couple you and Alton make, how capable you are, how hard-workin' Alton is. If Will saw it—and you know how blind to such things men can be—it must be pretty obvious to the others." Fanny chuckled. "When even Will remarks about Alton bein' smitten, then you can rest assured the big galoot's head over heels in love with you!"

Sue Ellen's cheeks flamed. Nervously her eyes darted around the room, seeking shelter from Fanny's knowing gaze. Sue Ellen had suspected how Alton felt, just as in her heart she recognized her growing feelings for him—feelings she knew were not right for her to have for a man like Alton. Especially with Nathan not yet in his grave a year.

"Fanny, I'm a widow. Just since last December."

"I know that, honey," Fanny soothed, "but that doesn't stop you from being a woman. I know you still grieve. Any woman would. But someday you'll feel for another man what you felt for Nathan. It's plain that Alton is hopin' that when that day comes, he'll be the man you'll choose."

"I like Alton," Sue Ellen admitted. "He's a good man. And Lord knows how grateful I am for all he's done for us. Maybe I even love him, Fanny," Sue Ellen confessed shamelessly, "but it's not the kind of love I want—the kind I must have to marry again." Sue Ellen's voice dropped low with pain. "Alton's not the man I need him to be . . . and I fear the day I'm forced to tell him that."

"Maybe you won't have to, Sue. With time, the Lord can make Alton into a new person."

"Even though it's bold of me to admit it, Fanny, I hope you're right. I'm praying you're right."

"We all are, honey." Fanny patted Sue Ellen's arm, then stood to go when Will called her to the wagon. Reaching the doorway, Fanny turned. "Be patient and understanding, Sue. If ever there was a man in need of a gentle, compassionate woman, it's Alton. He loves you, girl. A love as strong as his can't be all bad. Trust the Lord to make it into something better."

chapter
4

AFTER A DAY or two of sulking, Alton shook off the remnants of his jealousy and reverted to his usual good humor.

The farm flourished under his care as did young Jem. There was no need to coax or cajole the boy to help him with the chores, for Jem labored tirelessly, emulating the tall, strong man he had come to admire.

Now, neat rows of corn marched through the fields, their bright green banners waving nearer the sun each day. Firewood was stacked in ricks close to the house. A few loose stones in the cellar had been repaired, and shelves built for Sue Ellen's preserves.

Experiencing contentment unlike any he'd ever known, Alton gave no further thought to leaving. Home for him now was Salt Creek—and Sue Ellen.

Sue Ellen spoke often about that God of hers, explaining how the Lord has a reason and purpose for everything that happens to folks—the good and the bad. It pleased Alton to hope that she was right and that maybe God had brought them together for a reason—for Sue Ellen to become his wife and to mother the children Alton had dreamed would someday be his.

She wanted more children—he was sure of it, for he'd

noticed the secret hunger in her eyes when she shared the joys of Lizzie Childers' waiting, and he'd spied the intricate design she was creating for a baby quilt.

During the coming days Alton spent every free moment helping Will and Harmon prepare lumber for the barn raising. In the evenings, after her chores were done, Sue Ellen kept her needles flying on the quilt for Lizzie's baby, while Jem visited neighbors or fished in Salt Creek, catching carp and catfish to supplement their meals.

June slipped quickly by.

On the warm summer evenings when the humidity made sleeping impossible, Alton moved the rough-hewn chairs he'd built for Sue Ellen to a spot outside under the stars. The three of them would sit in comfortable silence, listening to the whippoorwill cry from his hiding place in the rail fence and watching the fireflies dance across the summer sky.

July attacked with savage heat.

"We're plannin' the barn raisin' for the Fourth," Alton told Sue Ellen one sultry night when he came in, drenched with perspiration. "All the neighbors will be there, so we should be done by nightfall. We'll celebrate the barn—and Independence Day, too."

"That will be fun," Sue Ellen said, fanning herself with her apron.

"Harm's plannin' on holdin' a square dance in the barn—a real country hoedown," Alton continued. "Will's told all the fellers to bring their banjos, fiddles, mandolins, and whatever else they can play. Those who don't care to dance can enjoy the music."

"You'll take your harmonica?" Sue Ellen asked.

"Ummm . . . thought I might."

"Please do," Sue Ellen urged. "You know how everyone enjoys hearing you play."

"It'll be a big day. Lots of music and food, too, knowin' the womenfolk."

"I'll talk to Fanny about that. I surely want to do my share."

That night a summer storm broke the drought and left the air light and clear.

"Your prayers for good weather have been answered, Sue," Alton said when he brought the team around the morning of the barn raising and helped Sue Ellen carry items to the wagon. "Did you ever see sech a pretty day?"

By the time Alton and the Stones arrived at Lizzie and Harm Childers' place, the wagons were lined up all around. Children, like so many butterflies, flitted about, playing tag and hide-and-seek. Men swung tools, bucked crosscut saws, hefted timbers, pounded pegs, and used pans of water to level the building, adjusting timbers until the water remained even in the container. Horses panted with the strain of raising the heavy rafters. Women bustled around, forming makeshift plank tables, exchanging bits of news as they worked.

All morning the Childers' farm was aflutter with activity. By noon the rafters were silhouetted against the clear sky and the men broke from their work to eat.

Will Preston stood at the head of the long table to ask the blessing before the men filed through to heap their plates. Women hovered behind the table, ready to help the ravenous men feed appetites whetted by hard work and the pleasing aromas that had drifted on the breeze all morning.

The plank table groaned beneath the weight of sugar-cured hams, the meat bright red, the hide dark brown from sugar and hickory smoke. Crispy fried chicken surrendered to the touch, and noodles swimming in rich gravy flowed over mounds of mashed potatoes, yellow with fresh butter. Honey from a bee tree on a neighbor's farm melted and ran sweetly thin from the crisp cat-head biscuits, Fanny's specialty. Moist chocolate cake, separated with light frosting between the layers, vied with flaky fruit pies, cookies, and sugared doughnuts.

After the men were finished, the women served the children. When they sent their young off to play, they filled their own plates. Still, food remained. Plenty for the evening meal.

"I haven't enjoyed myself so much in years!" Fanny announced, lifting her apron to fan her warm face. "And to think the day's little more than begun—with a party planned for tonight!"

"I hope the men won't be too tired to enjoy themselves," worried one young woman. "I know my young'uns will be if I don't see to it they nap under the wagon this afternoon."

"The men will be tired," Fanny nodded, "but probably no more so than we'll be after layin' out two big meals."

Chuckling, the women agreed, and set about clearing up the leftovers. Chatter turned to plans for preparing the evening meal, to allow plenty of time to tidy up before the party.

The sun was skimming the horizon, slowly sinking behind the trees, when the men let out a chorus of whoops. Harm drove the last peg into the barn. It was finished!

"Here they come!" Fanny Preston cried and clanged the iron dinner bell.

Following the words of thanksgiving, the men made fast work of the reheated platters of food. When their appetites were satisfied, the children, some silent and still sleepy from their naps, lined up to eat. Then the women quickly picked at their food, before rushing to pack away what remained of the day's feast.

Before the last table covering was folded and put away, the men began tuning their instruments. Harm Childers produced an empty nail keg and handed Lizzie's little brother a stick, creating a drum. Alton got out his harmonica, blew a few trial notes, then joined the band. His reception was so enthusiastic that he warmed to the occasion, grew bold, and wildly improvised with trilling notes.

"Is there anything you can't do, Alton?" teased one man, clapping him on the shoulder.

Alton grinned. "I can't cook 'n' I can't sew. But don't you worry ... I'll marry me a woman who can!"

The members of the band took their places. Will's youngest, Rory, studiously thumped the nail keg to mark the beat. The fiddles squawked and screeched while banjos added plucky harmony. Above the blend of background music, Alton's harmonica sang a sweet, mournful solo, the notes rising clear and true, wavering, fading, then bursting forth anew.

As the laborers drew their second wind, several of the younger men cautiously approached shy, blushing girls to lead them through a rollicking, foot-stomping square dance. Will called instructions, weaving them in and out of the formations until they were out of breath.

"Isn't this fun?" cried Lizzie, looking on.

"Yes," agreed Sue Ellen, "and it's high time, too!"

Lizzie broke into a helpless grin when she looked across the barn that was softly illuminated in the golden glow of many coal oil lanterns hung from nails driven into posts. "I don't know who's havin' more fun—," she said, giggling, "my pa or your Alton."

Sue Ellen followed Lizzie's gaze. Alton, his blue eyes sparkling, panted for breath between runs on his harmonica.

He sat on a stump of oak, thumping his foot to the rhythm of the music.

"The band's swell, ain't it?" Lizzie sighed. She glanced at her gently blossoming figure, still neatly concealed beneath the roomy apron. "Kind of makes me wish I could dance, Sue."

Sue Ellen smiled. "I know what you mean, honey," she said sympathetically. "There'll be time for that again, Lizzie . . . for both of us . . . when it won't be improper."

"Well, no one can gossip if I just tap my foot," Lizzie insisted stubbornly.

"And foot-tapping music it is, too," said Sue Ellen. "I haven't heard some of those old Civil War tunes in a long time. Truly, it's almost an effort not to tap or clap, isn't it?"

Throughout the evening Sue Ellen had caught herself stepping along smartly to the beat of the music as she fetched refreshments for her neighbors. The one time Sue Ellen had unconsciously yielded to the impulse to tap her toes beneath her long skirts, the motion hadn't been lost on Alton.

Every time he got the chance, he had watched her and his heart swelled and fairly ached with love. Love! Even the word brought a helpless smile to his face, and he knew at last he understood the meaning of the emotion. Though it was a feeling he couldn't describe, couldn't capture, he knew it was there, transforming every moment.

More than anything Alton itched to swing Sue Ellen through a square dance, bowing to his lady, promenading her home, seeing her face flush as a happy laugh escaped her lips. Alton sensed that was what Sue Ellen wanted, too.

Once when Alton had taken a break, she had served him cool cider and a piece of spice cake. He saw the affection and pride glowing in her eyes when she complimented him on his fine playing. Alton felt all warm inside. That a good and gentle woman like Sue Ellen Stone could find him worthy of respect and admiration was almost more than he could comprehend.

The music began again. Though Alton's notes were perfectly synchronized with those of the other musicians, his thoughts were across the barn with Sue Ellen. She'd seemed different, somehow, during the interlude. More alive. More vibrant. And never, never more beautiful. Behind the serenity of her eyes danced a sparkling glint of mischief, and it endeared her even more to Alton.

Almost as if someone had booted him off a log, Alton sprang from the stump block. He crossed the barn in long-legged strides, playing his harmonica as he approached Sue Ellen. Sensing his presence, Sue Ellen turned to confront Alton. Something in his eyes startled her.

Before Sue Ellen could protest, Alton gripped her wrist and tugged her from behind the booth. Lizzie's eyes widened in surprise and her hand flew to her mouth. Then, as Sue Ellen pulled back, Lizzie countered the movement by giving her a healthy shove in Alton's direction.

"*Lizzie!*" Sue Ellen cried, aghast.

Sue Ellen found herself in a square.

"Alton Wheeler, this is insane!" she cried. "Stop it this minute! Have you completely lost your reason?"

"Gentlemen, bow to your partners!" Will bawled. "Ladies, favor your man. All join hands and—"

Alton grinned as he took Sue Ellen's hand and circled her to the right. Sue Ellen's face scorched with embarrassment. She didn't know what to do. While she was trying to figure it out, she was led through the intricate routine.

"Havin' fun?" Alton grinned down at her.

Sue Ellen didn't know if she wanted to laugh or cry. Just

then Will called for them to switch partners and she was gone from Alton's side.

"How could you do this to me!" she cried when he was beside her again. "What are people going to think . . . a widow . . . dancing?"

Alton glanced at Lizzie's pleased smile as she watched the squares bloom like flowers—blossoming, dropping petals, budding, then blossoming again—as they moved in and out of step.

"Who cares what people think, Sue?" Alton removed the harmonica from his mouth to answer her.

"*I* care!" Sue Ellen fumed. "Now take me back to Lizzie!"

"Can't break up the square." Alton's hand imprisoned hers. "You may as well finish what you started."

"What *you* started, you mean! Alton, I could just, just—," she sputtered in impotent rage and embarrassment. Sue Ellen felt near tears. Or hysterical laughter. She wasn't sure which. She looked around at the blur of smiling faces. "What are people going to say?" she cried again.

Alton threw back his head and laughed as he crossed hands with hers and skipped her on home. He'd examined the faces of all their friends. Faces that revealed only approval—with nary the hint of a frown in sight.

"I'll tell you what they're sayin', Sue Ellen Stone. Our friends are thinkin' it's high time you forgot you were a widow . . . and remembered you're a woman!" he said as another man in the square moved to claim Sue Ellen for his temporary partner.

Alton moved to the side of a chubby matron, a grin splitting his features from ear to ear.

When the long day ended, Sue Ellen silently made her way to the wagon. Alton was unusually quiet at her side as if he were afraid to speak. Jem, unaware of the tension between them, clambered aboard, lay down in the wagon bed, and was almost instantly asleep. The horses plodded along, the lanterns looped to their collars lighting the way.

Alton had enjoyed the day from early morn to late evening. He sensed secretly that Sue Ellen had, too. But from the strange way she was carrying on, he feared he'd done something terribly wrong.

Although their friendship had sprung to life in the past few months, to Alton it seemed forever that he had been waiting, longing, for Sue Ellen to abandon her widow's weeds and signal to him that there was hope he might replace the lost affection in her life with love's fresh passion. But he couldn't rush her decision. Sue Ellen Stone was a woman worth waiting for. When she was ready to accept and return his love—he vowed to be there waiting.

"Sue," he finally spoke into the darkness, "I'm sorry if I done somethin' to make you unhappy. I guess I was moved by the moment." He cleared his throat. "Sometimes I'm impulsive like that."

She laughed softly. "I know."

"I never stopped to think it might upset you like it did. I never stopped to think that maybe you're one of them Christians that don't believe in dancin' and that I forced you to do something you feel is wrong. Did I?"

Sue Ellen smiled at the contrition in his voice. "No, nothing like that," she assured him.

"Oh. Well, I'm relieved then," Alton said, sighing. "But the way you was actin' . . . it did set me to thinkin'."

It had set Sue Ellen to thinking, too. The rest of the way home they silently pondered the situation. Sue Ellen had felt outraged when Alton yanked her from Lizzie's side. She'd suffered any number of painful emotions. Yet one emotion crowded out all the rest.

In Alton's arms she'd found the first true contentment and shred of lighthearted gaiety she'd known since Nathan died. She knew that she loved and wanted Alton—as surely as he did her. But her heavy heart throbbed with the aching realization that he was not a man with whom she could hope to have an enduring love, no matter how happy their present moments together.

Alton loved her now. But he was as wild and reckless as an untamed stallion—as unsettled as thistledown bandied on the breeze. She knew that without a solid commitment of faith like her own to help them weather the bad times, the fires of Alton's love might grow as cold as ashes.

chapter
5

THAT NIGHT Sue Ellen slept poorly, tossing and turning on the straw tick. It seemed she'd been asleep for only moments when the sun's slanting rays fell across her eyes, rousing her from her troubled rest.

Through the night, on his rude mat in the barn, Alton stared into the darkness. Images from the day haunted him. He wished he could buy back his behavior.

When the new day dawned, he was still wishing he could ransom away the memories even as he knew it was impossible. He dreaded facing Sue Ellen over breakfast, but he knew he would have to. Forcing himself to confront her calmly would make the embarrassment fade faster for both of them.

When Alton saw that there was no smoke drifting from the chimney, he decided to bide his time and do a few chores before seeing Sue Ellen.

Sue Ellen blinked her eyes open and noticed the full light outside her window—evidence that she'd slept longer than planned. Her bare feet hit the floor.

"Time to get up, son!" she called to Jem.

Sue Ellen pulled the quilts into order on her tick, dressed, quickly combed her hair, and rushed into the kitchen to begin their morning meal.

She yanked open the door of the cookstove. The handle was cool. The coals had died down, forming fluffy gray ashes, and she sighed when she realized how late breakfast would be.

"Jem, get up! I need some kindling!"

Jem crawled down the ladder from the loft. Sue Ellen took the dented coffeepot to the pump and filled it along with the water bucket. She set the pot on the cool stove.

Sue Ellen knelt and peered into the stove's sooty firebox. She grabbed the poker and began vigorously stirring through the ashes, raking the few orange coals into a small heap. In her haste, coals spilled over the lip of the firebox and became lost in the folds of her skirt. She jumped up, shaking her dress. A flame flared near the hem. She clutched it up and began beating at it.

Jem trooped into the cabin with kindling. When he saw the smoke, the flames, and smelled the scorching cotton, he dropped the kindling, grabbed the bucket of drinking water, and threw it, dipper and all, over his mother.

"Jem!" Sue Ellen shrieked as cold water dashed over her and puddled on the wood floor. Her dress clung wetly to her slim curves. "Oh, Jem—"

"I–I was only trying to . . ." Jem's words trailed off.

Sue Ellen felt near tears even as she realized the humor of her predicament.

"I know what you were doing, Jem, but the skirt wasn't burning that badly. See if you can do something about that fire, and mop the water from the floor. I'll have to change into something dry."

Sue Ellen made a wet trail to her room and peeled off the soggy dress. The holes in the skirt were worse than she'd realized. It would take painstaking mending before it would be fit to wear again. Even then it would only be suitable for working around the farm. Sighing, Sue Ellen reached for the peg where her other dress hung. Her fingers closed on thin air. It wasn't there!

Then she remembered the barn raising. She hadn't had time to do the wash the day before. After a day spent baking pies for the barn raising, that dress was so smudged with flour and grime she couldn't possibly wear it.

Helplessly Sue Ellen looked around her. Her eyes fell on the trunk containing the beautiful green dress. She chewed her lip and opened the lid. Smoothing the dress across her bed, she made a quick decision and slipped it over her head. As soon as she got the chance, she vowed, she'd buy some dark material and make mourning dresses fit to wear visiting. Until then she'd have to stay home. And be very careful with the few dark dresses she had to wear.

Jem looked up from the gently blazing fire when Sue Ellen entered the kitchen.

"Ma!" His brown eyes revealed shock.

Sue Ellen flushed and avoided his eyes. "I had to put on something," she said in quiet defense. "It's the only clean dress I had."

"I didn't mean that, Ma. It's only that . . . you look mighty nice."

"I have to wear this dress . . . but only for today," she promised.

Jem's concern rested elsewhere. "Will breakfast be ready soon? Or should I check my trot line on the creek first?"

"Don't run off. It won't take long to get the griddle hot enough for flapjacks. Alton loves them, and they're quick." Sue Ellen glanced out the window. "He should be here soon."

Almost on the heels of her words, Alton arrived. He hesitated in the doorway to adjust to the change in light.

When he saw Sue Ellen, his blue eyes softened. Sue Ellen felt her cheeks grow warm under his intense scrutiny, and she served the breakfast without comment.

Alton, for his part, was silent, too. No words came to him. He was too enmeshed in his thoughts to speak. And the more he mulled it all over, the higher his spirits soared.

After his rash words the night before—words he'd come to regret—he now saw things in a better light. Starting with the fact that Sue Ellen had fixed his favorite breakfast—flapjacks.

Not only that, but she was wearing the bright-colored dress—the one he'd told her someday she'd want to wear again. He looked at Sue Ellen, lovely in the dainty frock, and he interpreted it as a sign that she had taken to heart his words of the night before. He saw it as proof that she conceded he was right. That it was high time she forgot she was a widow and remembered she was a woman. The kind of genteel woman Sue was, Alton knew she couldn't very well just up and tell him. She'd put on the dress and *show* him!

Sue Ellen was self-conscious and quiet during the meal, but Alton was too absorbed in his plans to notice. When Jem excused himself to go check his lines on the creek, Alton and Sue Ellen lingered over the last of the coffee in the pot.

Alton's mind was whirling. Sue Ellen was ideal for him! He couldn't believe his luck in loving her and being loved by her. The way he felt, Alton wanted everything to be perfect when he asked her to become his wife, and his thoughts skipped ahead to institute his plans.

"It sure was a nice day yesterday," he said finally, "'n' the weather promises to be as good today. Makes it sort of hard fer a feller to set his mind on work."

"Doesn't it, though?" Sue Ellen agreed. "And I've got so much to do."

"I thought I'd take a walk to the corn patch to see how it's doin'. It's probably shot up a foot after the last little rain."

"Jem remarked about it, too."

Alton hesitated. "Would you care to walk along, Sue?" he invited, heart thudding.

Sue Ellen paused, frowning. "If it won't take too long," she agreed. "I've got all of yesterday's work waiting and today's as well."

She stacked the dishes in the metal pan and set a kettle of water on the stove to heat before following Alton from the cabin. Talk between them came easy. Both relaxed and seemed determined to put behind them the strain of the night before. Alton purposely slowed his strides to match Sue Ellen's steps.

Crows hovered overhead, arching and dipping with the wind's currents. A redbird sang from the top of a tree. Katydids cried from their hiding places in the long grass. The pigs in their pen grunted contentedly as the couple passed by.

"The corn sure is shootin' up," Alton murmured and touched a stalk where the ear of grain would soon be filling out with plump kernels. "We'll be needin' more rain."

"If weather's fit, we'll have a good crop," Sue Ellen ventured an opinion.

Alton nodded. "Plenty fer the livestock, some to grind fer meal, and enough to set back fer next year's seed."

Alton turned from the small field and strolled to the nearby woods. Sue Ellen followed. A pile of firewood was stacked to be hauled to the cabin and ricked as time allowed.

"You've been so good for my boy, Alton," Sue Ellen said softly.

He slowed to examine a blackberry, still hard and red but on its way to ripening a deep purple. Casually he plucked another wildflower to add to the clump clutched in his hand.

"Well, it's no secret I like the boy," he replied.

"Jeremiah's papa was kept so busy with the company business that sometimes neither Jem nor I saw much of him. I'm grateful to you for being like a pa to a fatherless boy."

Alton turned to face Sue Ellen. Now that the moment he'd been scheming and planning for had arrived, his heart was hammering wildly. Awkwardly he thrust the fistful of wildflowers into her hands.

"I—I'd like to be more than just 'like a pa' to your boy, Sue," he stammered. "I'd like to become his real pa. I'd be proud to claim Jem as my son." His voice lowered to a fervent whisper. "Prouder still to have you fer my wife."

Alton's eyes met Sue Ellen's. Her complexion flushed rose and the breath caught in her throat. Full, soft lips trembled, struggling to give voice to swirling thoughts, but no sound came.

Hesitantly Alton took a step toward Sue Ellen. When she did not retreat, indeed seemed to sway toward him, he took another. And another. Before he knew it—before she knew it—Sue Ellen was in his arms.

She looked up into his eyes with soft surprise. Alton wasn't sure if he tilted Sue Ellen's chin up, or if she lifted her lips to his in sweet surrender.

"Oh, Sue, Sue!" Alton whispered feverishly. His lips tasted hers and he sighed with utter contentment.

Alton breathed her name over and over. Strong hands held her gently to him. He thrilled to the innocence of her mouth and the chaste beauty that stirred such protective, loving feelings in him. Feelings far beyond mere physical desire.

Clumsily Alton patted Sue Ellen, unsure exactly how to proceed with a virtuous woman. A woman he not only desired—but cherished.

She yielded to his embrace, resting her cheek against his broad chest as he stroked her thick, luxurious hair and stared over the top of her head at the vine-covered cabin. He'd been alone all his life, but he'd never be so alone again. Not with Sue Ellen at his side.

A few times Alton had searched for something he sensed was missing from his life. Failing to find it, he'd quit looking. But now he realized that he'd been looking in all the wrong places. All the painted women he'd known and held in his arms had never felt quite right. Not like Sue Ellen who already seemed a natural part of him.

Once more Alton brought his lips down the mere fraction of an inch it took to capture Sue Ellen's kiss. His heart skipped to a wild beat when instead of demurely standing in his embrace, Sue Ellen wrapped her own soft arms around his neck, pressed against him, and returned his kiss with a passion that matched his own.

"Sue Ellen— Oh, Sue! I love you, woman. I swear I do. How I love you."

"And I love you, Alton."

Despite the warm sunlight that enveloped them, Sue Ellen suddenly shivered in his arms. Looking up at him, she saw her desire mirrored in his eyes.

"Marry me, Sue Ellen. Please marry me. Let me take care of you always. I want to be your man."

"Alton—"

Slowly, released from the captivating emotions of the moment, Sue Ellen's reason returned. While her heart begged her to say yes, she knew she must resist.

"You can wear this dress," Alton was saying. "There'll be green ribbons for your hair. You'll be the prettiest bride ever to walk on earth!"

"Alton—" Sue Ellen's voice was faint, choking. "I—I *can't* marry you."

Sue Ellen's words cleaved the still air like a whiplash. Alton stared dumbly at her. His lips parted, but no words were immediately forthcoming.

79

"But—but . . . you just said you loved me," he spoke in a dazed tone. "I—I don't understand."

Sue Ellen stared miserably at the wildflowers that drooped in her hand. Moments ago they'd been as fresh as new love when Alton gave them to her. Now they wilted with what seemed a despair as deep as her own.

"You can't ask me to forget Nathan so soon. Why, it hasn't even been a year since I buried him. What would people think?"

"They'd understand," Alton murmured gently. "We've got dandy neighbors, Sue. They like us. They wouldn't say things to hurt us. I'm not asking you to forget the past, only beggin' you to look toward the future. Many a marriage has been rushed on a bit when a widow woman needed the protection of a man."

Sue Ellen seemed shaken by his words. In her eyes he saw proof that she wanted him, in spite of all her reservations.

Alton took her in his arms again and kissed her until Sue Ellen shivered with pleasure and her fingers uncurled to drop the wilted flowers in order that she might embrace him more fully.

How she desired to accept him as her husband. She needed him. She wanted him. But one small part of her woman's heart reminded her that her own desires mattered little. She had made another sacred vow long ago, and it was this that overshadowed all else.

Alton was the first to break away. His blue eyes seemed almost savage with mysterious emotions. He gripped her soft shoulders.

"Marry me, Sue Ellen Stone," he ordered in a hoarse whisper.

Sue Ellen shook her head, her eyes misty with tears. "I want to," she groaned. "Oh, I want to . . . but I can't."

"I'll wait for you, Sue, if I have to," he promised. "I'll wait and wait . . . if you'll just agree to be mine."

"There's no sense wasting time waiting . . . or hoping. I can't *ever* marry you, Alton." She dropped her head in anguish.

"*Can't?*" he questioned in a strangled voice. "Or *won't?*"

"Oh, Alton, please don't make me say it."

"Say what?"

She bit her lip and turned away, staring into the dense woods, yet seeing nothing but his tortured face.

"You're a proud man, Alton Wheeler," she said. "Too proud to know that you need the Lord as your Savior." Somehow she found the strength to press the words past her lips. "My husband, Jem's father, must be a man of God like the Good Book says. Please . . . you have to understand!"

Alton forced her to face him. His complexion faded before her eyes, then grew red with anger.

"That's the most blame-fool, silly notion I've ever heard, Sue Ellen Stone! You can't be serious!"

"But I am," she said miserably.

Alton searched her eyes. He saw no hint of levity there. The world swayed dizzily around him, and an ugly bitterness rose in the pit of his stomach, burning until he thought he'd be consumed by it.

"So that's it," he spat, the words whistling from between clenched teeth. "After all I've done for you, suddenly I'm not good enough." His eyes grew flat and hard. "Some dandified, weak sister like what's-his-name you met at the social, is good enough. But me . . . who's sweated, toiled, and wore blisters on his hands . . . I ain't?"

Alton started to curse. Oaths he hadn't used in a long time spewed from his lips. He turned away, shoulders sagging, as he choked on the words. His tears were restrained only by fiery rage.

Sue Ellen stared at him in mute agony. Unable to hear more, she clutched her skirts to her and hurried toward the cabin. She was stung by the things he'd uttered—cruel, hurtful, ugly, untrue things, spoken in anger. She felt ill when she recalled her own awkward explanation and realized how deeply she had hurt him.

The cabin door banged shut behind her. Sue Ellen threw herself across the bed and cried as if her heart would break. The crackling straw tick did little to muffle her sobs.

Always she'd tried to follow the Lord's path and do His will. Never before had it felt so wrong or hurt so much to do something that she knew she had to do.

At last Sue Ellen dried her eyes and prayed for wisdom to explain her true feelings to Alton—the hard truth that, though she loved him as she knew he loved her, without a mutual commitment to Christ, Alton could never offer her quite enough.

Then she prayed for his injured pride, for healing for the hurt she had inflicted. Above all, she prayed for Alton himself and for his relationship with the Lord. Alton reminded her so much of Peter—that brawny fisherman who followed Jesus— so proud, so unbending, so impetuous. Yet after Peter met Jesus, he was never again the same. Oh, how she yearned for Alton to learn that admitting his need for the Lord would not make him less manly—but more of a man.

Already her heart lifted with the hope that Peter's experience might become Alton's. Sue Ellen raised her face from the tear-dampened pillow. Surely there were no tears left. Silently she made her way to the kitchen, wet a cloth in the basin, and touched it to her face. She closed her eyes against the cool dampness. Then startled, flipped them open, when she heard the soft clops on the dusty path and the jingling of harness bells.

Sue Ellen crossed the cabin with quick steps and threw

open the door. There sat Alton, unyielding as stone, on the spring seat of the wagon with all of his belongings bundled behind him.

He was leaving! *Leaving!*

The realization struck Sue Ellen a crippling blow. Gasping, she flung herself from the cabin and stumbled across the grassy knoll. She clutched a giant tree for support, gripping the rough bark as she stared after the man she loved. Tears coursed a scalding trail down her cheeks.

Pitifully she cried his name. But Alton couldn't hear her. Or *wouldn't!*

Sue Ellen was almost blind with tears when he turned onto the main trail. She saw him lash the horses, saw the Clydesdales break into a full gallop.

"Wait!" Sue Ellen screamed. "Please wait!"

He didn't slow. Helplessly she followed with her eyes until he was lost to her sight by the woodland between them. Numb, drained, she turned to the cabin. Alton was gone. Gone! And unless it was God's will—she would never see him again.

Sue Ellen's eyes were red and swollen when Jem returned home with a burlap bag weighted with fish to be cured in brine and smoked for the winter ahead.

"Where's Alton?" he asked. "I could use some help cleaning these fish."

Sue Ellen avoided Jem's eyes. "He's gone."

"Gone? Gone where? To town?" When Jem drew near, Sue Ellen had no choice but to face him. He saw her ravaged face and he understood. "Oh, Ma, no!" Jem's voice shook.

"He left this morning."

"F—for good?" Jem asked, seeing the answer in his mother's eyes.

Sue Ellen nodded. "It looks that way, Jeremiah."

Jem, who'd tried so hard to be brave for his ma's sake, felt his lip tremble. He bit down, hard. So hard the skin split. But it did no good. He gulped, lost control, and flung himself into Sue Ellen's arms, sobbing. She patted his thin shoulders and blinked back the tears that burned in her own eyes.

"H—how could Alton leave us, Ma? I thought he loved us, too. Oh, Ma . . . how could he?"

"Shhhhh. Shhhhh. Alton does love us, Jem. He thought the world of you. Alton would've admired to have you for his son. He left in anger. But behind that fury, Jem, love's still there. Maybe someday Alton will come back to us. He may not return soon. Or even at all. But if he returns, it'll be God's will and in love's own time."

"We'll make it, Ma," Jem said. "Alton taught me a lot. Almost everything I need to know to take care of you so we can get through the winter."

Sue Ellen hugged Jem before she turned back to her work.

That night after supper, when the loneliness seemed sharpest, soft hoofbeats fell on the path to the cabin. Sue Ellen's heart skipped a beat. Her eyes flew to seek Jem's. Wordlessly they rushed to the door.

"It's only Fanny and Will, Ma," Jem said, sighing.

"Let's go meet them, son. Be neighborly. Don't let your disappointment show."

Will wrapped the rein leathers in place and turned to help his stout wife from the seat while their son tumbled off the back.

"Is Alton around somewhere?" Will asked after greeting Sue Ellen.

She forced a smile. "No, he's gone. Left this morning," she explained in a light voice.

"I didn't know he was planning a trip to town, or I'd have asked him to pick me up a few—"

Fanny touched his arm.

"Will! Didn't you have something you had to show Jem 'n' our young'un?" she cut in pointedly.

Her tall husband gave her a befuddled look, started to speak, then thought better of it. But he gave Jem a curious look before jerking his head to signal for the lad and his own son to follow him.

Fanny's brown eyes were large and luminous with sympathy. Her plump arms enfolded Sue Ellen tenderly.

"Oh, Sue—I'm sorry. I'm so very sorry."

The older woman's kind voice, heavy with sympathy, was all it took.

Like from a bottle uncorked, Sue Ellen's tears flooded. She burrowed into Fanny's solid, comforting warmth and cried as Fanny patted her.

"I know you love him, Sue Ellen. And I understand why you can't accept his love. Alton's a good man. God knows all the neighbors admire and adore that scamp. But he's like a wild stallion—needs gentlin'. You aren't strong enough to tame a fellow like Alton, but there's One who is. When he comes back, Alton will be a man after your heart, a man you won't hesitate givin' your love to. He'll be back," she promised. "I know it sure as I'm standin' here with breath in my body."

"I—I'm not so sure—," Sue Ellen whispered. "I've never seen him so hurt, so furious—"

"He'll get over it," Fanny predicted. "Alton may have been fit to explode when he left. He has human emotions, hot 'n' strong. But they'll pale in the face of a stronger emotion—the strongest of all. The love of God . . . and a good woman."

chapter
6

ALTON'S HEART was heavy with the weight of Sue Ellen's unexpected, puzzling refusal. Numb with grief and rage, he didn't allow himself time to think as he scrambled around the crude, musty quarters he'd arranged in the barn and threw his belongings into a heap on the back of the wagon, whistling for the horses. They stood quietly in place while he quickly hitched them to their harnesses.

Alton was tempted to abandon the quilt Sue Ellen had given him. Leave it lying in a heap on the dirt floor for her to find. In his anger and hurt, he wanted no part of her. But his pragmatic nature won out. He knew he'd need the warm comforter to shield him against chilly nights ahead.

"I earned it—every stitch of it," he growled under his breath as he threw it onto the wagon. He wouldn't let himself admit that in a tiny corner of his heart he wanted this memento of the one decent woman who'd entered his life— the beautiful woman who'd given him as much joy as she had caused him agony.

Alton lunged onto the seat, yanked the reins, and lashed the horses ahead. Stoically he refused to glance toward the cabin when he left. He knew he couldn't bear it if his eyes fell on Sue Ellen Stone once more. Brutally he whipped Doc and

Dan on, racing from the farm as fast as he could. Looking neither right nor left, Alton was blind to anything but the dusty brown path immediately ahead.

As he passed Will and Fanny's farm, Alton sat motionless as a granite boulder. He didn't want to chance seeing Will at work in the field and be expected to rein in the team to pass the time of day. It would be less painful for them both if Will Preston looked up, waved, and thought Alton's lack of response was an oversight, not intentional.

With each mile that fell between Alton and the Union Township area he'd come to love, the agony in his heart eased, to be replaced by chilling confusion.

At the farm, Alton had faced each day content and comfortable, thinking no further ahead than the next sunrise. Suddenly he found his thoughts tumbling from one possibility to another. Alton didn't know now where his future lay, for the one thing he wanted above all else—Sue Ellen—was beyond his reach. The truth was—and it stung afresh—that she wouldn't have him.

When Alton came to the crossroad after fording the creek, he gave the horses free rein to choose their path. The road to Effingham was familiar; the way to Fiddler's Ridge was not. They plodded instinctively toward the county seat town.

As Alton passed through Effingham, he was tempted to stop for the day but resisted the idea. The town was too close to the source of his pain, and he feared that he'd cast aside all his pride, crawl on his hands and knees to Sue Ellen, and beg her to take him back. But he wouldn't humble himself like that for—for *anyone!*

A dull ache spread through the big man, underscored by the shooting pains that rippled up his spine each time the wagon bounced on the red brick street. East to Teutopolis and Indiana far beyond? Or west toward Altamont, the Mississippi River, and St. Louis, Missouri?

The horses, heads bobbing, swerved west.

Alton felt no relief or joy when familiar landmarks appeared. Always before, the route to St. Louis had filled him with admiration for the craggy hills, broad valleys, deep ravines, and towering timberland broken by creeks and fields. It was a journey that always sparked his thoughts with bright expectation. This time, however, he was filled with a strange sense of dread.

As he pondered the reason, he understood why. On Sue Ellen's farm he had come to enjoy serenity and peace. He had tasted a good way of life, and he still hungered for the lifestyle he had abandoned on her Salt Creek farm.

Like a distant, hazy memory that gains clarity the longer it is considered, his old life came back to him. But the past days spent gambling in ornate saloons, with random escapades to plush bawdy houses, paled in comparison to life with Sue Ellen.

Nevertheless, it seemed inevitable that he return to the life he'd known before. Indeed, there was nowhere else to turn.

Alton traveled for days. The wooden wagon wheels rolled over the miles as he crossed flat plains, skittered down hills, strained to the tops of knolls, and looked down upon the spreading valleys below.

Some nights he slept in hotels; others, he camped beside the wagon, turning the horses free of their harnesses, knowing they would not wander off.

Alton and his team were weary when they arrived in St. Louis. Old friends, old ways, and the old life beckoned.

He stabled the horses in a local livery. Then, as if drawn by a magnet, Alton found himself heading to a favorite haunt, the Idle Hour Saloon. Tinkling honky-tonk music spilled into the street to be heard two blocks away. The closer he came, the louder grew the laughter. Alton pushed his way into the brightly lit establishment. Several patrons turned to regard him curiously.

A few, their eyes widening with recognition, hailed him. "Look who's here! Come on over, you scoundrel, and let me buy you a drink!"

"Don't try to talk me into bettin' on the turn of a card, Alton. You fleeced me out of the last dollar you'll ever take from me to line your pockets!"

Laughter swelled. The warm welcome eased some of the cold, aching loneliness of Sue Ellen's rejection. Alton allowed himself to be led to the bar, smiling, answering their questions with half-truths. Somehow he managed to withhold the real facts about his whereabouts for the past few months, and his pals accepted his evasive comments without question.

The memory of Sue Ellen, even blighted by hurt as it was, was too precious to be tarnished by barroom speculation. These hard-bitten men would not understand what he felt for such a woman. They knew and understood only one kind. No, better not to mention her at all.

A painted lady in a tight dress came toward him, an inviting sway in her walk. Her musky perfume enveloped him, and her sultry voice and tinkling laughter washed over him like a warm wave. Alton shivered at the touch of her delicate hand on his forearm, and his reaction encouraged her.

She looped her arm through his, pressed close to him, and made gay chatter, while Alton downed the drinks bought by old cronies to welcome him back into their fold. The woman, sensing Alton was carrying a sizable wad of money, clung to him, plying him with laughter and caresses.

Eventually a couple of old friends persuaded Alton to take the empty seat at the poker table. The cards fell together with a soft swish each time the dealer fanned the deck. Five cards spun into the air, landing before the players. Charlotte, the girl from the bar, never left Alton's side, smiling vacantly over his shoulder at the cards in his hand.

Alton played the game lifelessly. Before, his enthusiasm had been tireless. Now, even when he won, the old thrill was gone. As he raked in crumpled greenbacks, silver and coppers, he was not thinking of the luxuries he could buy but translated the money into tools, corn, barbed wire, and goods needed for the farm.

In the past Alton had always won enough to stay ahead of the game and to pay his keep. He had never been forced to labor. If he grew bored with saloon life and desired a change of scenery, he took a trip on a river barge or mule train. It had been an easy, indolent existence.

Startling as it was, Alton discovered poker now bored him—even when the hands dealt almost made Charlotte gasp and promised him easy victory and even easier money.

He sighed and shifted on the chair. Eager to please, Charlotte massaged the tense muscles at the back of his neck.

The new bartender, Archie, smiled with approval, then moved from behind the shiny counter with its bottles lining the backbar. He rounded a corner—out of sight but not hearing—and bawled up the stairway for a girl to come down and get to work. Alton scarcely gave him a glance when the bartender returned to freshen their drinks. He was already feeling the effects of the whiskey he'd consumed, more than he really cared to drink, but he had accepted rather than risk insulting the friends who had treated him.

When Alton raked in the pot, winning yet again, he scraped his chair away from the small table. Charlotte swished her ruffled skirt aside.

"What's the matter, darlin'?" she asked. "Tired of playin'

already? I'm surprised at you quittin', handsome, while I was bringin' you such luck."

Alton smiled. "No offense to you, Miss Charlotte," he murmured. "But I'm tired from a long trip." He pressed some crumpled greenbacks into her warm hand. "Since you brought the luck, I'll share the rewards with you."

She looked at the money, more than she'd expected, and squealed with delight, plastering several quick kisses on Alton's bearded cheek.

"Are you wantin' me to go to your room with you, honey, to help you get—settled in?" she asked coyly.

"No thanks, Miss Charlotte," he refused, with a polite smile. "Wouldn't want to take away the good luck you're bound to bring some other feller. Don't doubt when I leave, they'll all fight for the honor of you standin' beside 'em."

"You silver-tongued devil," Charlotte laughed, delighted. "Maybe the reason you had such luck is because you're such a sweetheart."

"More'n likely it's because he's so seasoned with the cards," one of the losers grumped, then smiled as be beckoned Charlotte to his side and squeezed her hand as she brushed close to him.

"Audry! You no-good wench, get yourself down here before I lose my patience and drag you down. It's time to get to work, girl!" Archie, the bartender bawled. He turned around, almost smacking into Alton.

"Breakin' in bargirls," he said with a snort of anger, "is enough to break a man's spirit. What I ever did to deserve this—" He shook his head in disgust as words failed him. Then, as Alton leaned against the bar, Archie recited his troubles.

His best girls had quit, leaving him with Charlotte, an old

hand at the saloon business, as dependable as they came. One other, Belle, had her good days and her bad ones.

"Most girls do as I tell 'em and when I tell 'em. 'Cept this last one." He shook his head. "Has the face of an angel and the temperament of a mule!" Alton laughed. Archie gave him a hard look. "That's what I get for takin' in an ignorant country girl. She's straight off the farm and green as new-mown hay."

"I'd like to rent a room," Alton said, when Archie seemed ready to forget his irritations and get down to business.

"No problem, friend," he said, registering Alton and taking his money.

Alton sensed rather than saw the girl enter the saloon. When his eyes were drawn to her, she gave him a faltering smile as she meekly made her way to the bar.

"'Bout time you put in an appearance, Audry," Archie said in a grim tone, producing Alton's room key.

Alton noticed that the slim blonde flinched at the rancor in Archie's tone.

"Wh-what is it you want me to do, Archie?" she asked in a plaintive voice.

"See what I mean?" he spoke to Alton, ignoring the girl's question. "You have to tell 'em every move to make." Then he turned on Audry. "See Charlotte over there?" She nodded. "Well, go and do what she's doin'. Flirt with the men. Make sure they have a good time and make 'em feel that they don't want the good timin' to end when the bar closes. They can continue right on upstairs. Get the idea?"

"Yes, Archie."

When the girl walked away to do his bidding, Archie gave her a sharp smack across the bottom—more a caress than a spank. Alton saw her face color hotly and the quick tears spring to her eyes, clinging to her long lashes.

Suspecting she wasn't much over seventeen, Alton felt her pain and shame.

"Here's your key, Bub. The room's on the second floor, turn right, halfway down the hall. It's got everything you need." The bartender hesitated. "'Cept a woman for the night. Ain't none of the gals spoke for yet. You can take your pick."

Alton started to refuse. Then he saw the crimson color heighten in Audry's cheeks as she attempted to mimic Charlotte's light banter and bawdy manner.

Alton's lips were dry, and he licked them with the point of his tongue. He wasn't even sure what made him speak.

"Yeah, that'd be right nice, I reckon."

The bartender rubbed his hands together as he scanned the bar. "Which one will it be?" Archie asked, trying to contain his eagerness to make another easy dollar.

"That one—Audry—I think you said."

Archie looked surprised, then pleased. "She's a little spitfire, she is, but you look man enough to handle her. Teach the wench her place in this world, by golly! Audry!" he bellowed.

The girl stiffened, flinching as she faced him. Her eyes revealed that she expected criticism.

"C'mere, dolly," the bartender ordered. "This—uh—gentleman needs to be shown to his room." She nodded, looking relieved to leave the saloon for even a few minutes. "And when you get there," Archie said slowly, deliberately, "stay there. For the night." The girl's face blanched. "It's time you started earnin' your keep."

The relief she'd exhibited when called away from the boisterous card game turned to an expression of pure dread. Taking a deep breath, the girl led Alton to the staircase. He touched her elbow, steadying her. She seemed about ready to shake off his touch as something loathsome. But when she turned, she read the gentleness in his eyes. Almost dazed, a smile flitted briefly into place.

Mutely she showed Alton to his room, then self-consciously closed the door and locked it behind them. Alton stowed his few belongings, whistling a shrill tune. Silence stretched between them.

Requesting the girl for the night had seemed the right thing to do at the time, Alton realized, but now it seemed so wrong. Audry paced the room like a nervous filly in a corral. He noticed from her profile that her lower lip trembled. He thought about dismissing her. But to what? Archie's railings? Better she stay with him.

Finally she turned, glaring, her eyes flashing as her fists knotted at her sides. "A—aren't you going to tell me what you want me to do?" she cried the agonized question. Then she waited, her face haunted but determined.

Alton's heart hammered. "I don't want you to do nothin', ma'am," he murmured.

She stared, licking her lip. "Then what'd you ask for me for?" she challenged.

Alton gave a grim laugh. "Don't rightly know the answer to that myself, ma'am. Fact is, I've been sittin' here askin' myself the same thing." He paused. "Guess it was because you looked so miserable. I wanted to spare you that . . . at least for tonight."

"It doesn't make much difference," she sighed. "There's always tomorrow. And the next day." Her voice was a mere whisper. "If you're not wantin' me, I'd best get back downstairs, or there'll be the devil to pay with Archie."

"Stay," Alton said.

She looked at him, instantly suspicious.

"Stay with me—'n' talk," Alton suggested. "An'—an' I'll pay you for your time so Archie won't know."

Audry stared at him. "You'd do that for me? Why?" She studied him curiously.

"Sometimes," Alton said, "a feller gets lonely—'n' wants a friend to talk to bad enough to pay for the privilege. Guess maybe tonight I'm a man needin' a woman's ear."

His tongue loosened by the liquor he'd consumed, Alton began talking—a rambling, disjointed account of his months with Sue Ellen. Occasionally Audry nodded or sighed sympathetically. Then, when Alton lapsed into a deep silence, she told him about her own life—the recent hurt of her grandmother's death, the uncertainty of her future with no one to protect her and no one to provide for her, the shame she felt in turning to one of the few ways women were able to support themselves in these parts.

Audry wasn't sure how long she'd talked before she glanced across the room from where she sat in the chair and saw that Alton had long since fallen asleep and was snoring softly.

Knowing Archie wouldn't be pestering her or yelling at her and that this big man's kindness had bought her a night of peace, she leaned her head back and closed her eyes, pondering the thought that maybe all men weren't crude, uncaring brutes, after all. Sensing that Alton Wheeler was a man of integrity and good as his word, she knew the money would be hers in the morning. Feeling somewhat protected, she fell asleep with a sense of unconcern almost like that she had known before Gran died.

The next morning Alton awakened early. Quietly he moved about the room, collecting his things. From his wallet he took out greenbacks and laid them on the dresser where the girl would be sure to find the payment later.

Alton stared down at her, studying her. In her sleep the girl looked soft and vulnerable. *If her grandma had lived,* he thought, *things might've worked out so much differently. It wasn't fair*.

He laughed bitterly but softly so as not to awaken her. Who said life is fair? Or that it had to be? He himself was living proof that it wasn't! He'd given his all and done the best he could. Instead of the appreciation he'd expected as his due, he'd met with rejection.

Alton looked at Audry, and a small part of his heart ached for her. But there was really little else he could do. The night before, hearing her tearful story and watching her furtively drying her eyes on the hem of her skirt, he'd almost impulsively asked her to marry him. It would have been a way to rescue her from the saloon life and fling away his own painful memories at the same time.

But he'd thought better of it almost immediately. Audry didn't deserve his pity, and she would have learned soon enough that no matter what she ever did, he'd never love her enough. Because his heart—all of it—belonged to Sue Ellen Stone.

Quickly Alton left the room, shut the door noiselessly behind him, and clattered down the stairs and out the front door of the Idle Hour. He checked on the horses, then passed the time on the street corner, watching people pass by. Later, much later, as honky-tonk music drifted out to be carried on the breeze, he turned in the opposite direction and entered a saloon without even bothering to notice which one. He planned not to go back to the Idle Hour. For some reason he wanted to remember Audry as she'd last appeared to him—a sweet, innocent young girl. He didn't want to sit helplessly by, witnessing her fall, along with his own.

Wherever he went, Alton found old friends or made new. He could always be coaxed into taking an empty chair at a poker table. He played until his mind grew dull. Only when his stomach rumbled without ceasing did he break to satisfy his hunger. Instead of returning to the saloon, he walked the quiet streets, checking into yet another hotel without even inquiring about the cost. With his winnings in his pocket, it made no difference.

The days blended into one week, then two. Alton was growing increasingly bored and dissatisfied. His poker buddies began to grate on his nerves. Their minds seemed riveted on such inconsequential things, and Alton realized how much he missed the thoughtful conversations he'd enjoyed with Will and other neighbors. He even missed the affectionate teasing of Fanny, who, in her own homespun way, was more attractive than all the voluptuous girls who masked their innermost feelings while flaunting their physical charms.

Alton had been in the area for slightly over two weeks before he awoke to take a good look at the city. Debris littered crowded alleyways. Buildings were wedged side by side so tightly that he pined for the wide open spaces of Sue Ellen's farm. Crows hiding in the cornfield. Wind whispering through the timber. Water riffling over rocks in the creek. Blackberry briars heavy with fruit swaying beneath the late summer sun.

Already Alton's sun-bronzed skin had faded to the pallor of a frog's belly. Honest labor had hardened him. Made him feel he possessed worth. With inactivity and easy living, he quickly suffered a sense of slack. Worse, he'd come to feel he was losing the self-respect he had gained in Sue Ellen's presence. With her, he'd become a decent man. Well, at least a better one, because she'd treated him like one. Until that awful day after the barn raising.

"Goin' to be at the saloon tonight, Al?" called an acquaintance as he passed on the street.

Alton whirled, jerked from his thoughts. "Huh? Oh, sure. Yup. I'll be there."

But as he stared at the littered street, the realization dawned that he wouldn't be returning to the saloon. Or poker. Or drink. Or bawdy women.

He was going to get work. An honest job. He'd worked for Sue Ellen—he could labor for another. Maybe, if luck was with him, another job in another place would come to seem as right for him as the Stones' farm on Salt Creek.

Alton left St. Louis just as soon as he could claim Doc and Dan and settle up the livery bill. He crossed back into Illinois, following rough roads that led to small townships and sprawling farms.

Since he'd decided to hunt down some kind of job, Alton decided the best approach was a direct one. Alton stopped at a farm or two and inquired. Eying the brawny man with respect, the farmers turned him down, always offering helpful suggestions. Emboldened by the recommendations, Alton proceeded toward a larger farm. The owner left his task to greet the big man.

"Some of your neighbors said you might be in need of a hired hand," Alton began.

The man folded his lips into a thin line and shook his head. "Crops are planted. It'll be a long time until harvest. I could use your horses, friend, but not you. Sorry."

"Well, thanks for your time," Alton said, clucking to the team.

"The coal mine's hirin'," the farmer called after him. "You might get on there if you're wantin' a job and aren't particular about the work."

"Which way's the mine?"

The farmer approached the wagon and gave him directions.

Alton tipped his hat and headed the team back down the long lane.

A half-hour later Alton entered the mining camp and tethered the horses. Hopping down from the wagon, he strode toward the weather-beaten building—hardly more than a shack—which served as the office. A clerk glanced up from his desk when Alton entered.

"And what can I do for you?"

"I'm wantin' a job," Alton said, pushing his cap to the back of his head. "A farmer told me you're hirin'."

"That we are. We can always use a big man with a strong back."

Alton couldn't believe the job was so easily his. "How soon can I start?"

"It's up to you," the clerk shrugged. "Today. Tomorrow. This is a company town. There's a place for you. I'll assign your quarters so you can get squared away in your shanty."

"Tomorrow then," Alton decided. "I've got things to attend to first."

"Good enough," the clerk agreed. "Have you ever worked a mine before?"

"No. Never."

He frowned. "Are you sure you can do it?" he asked a bit dubiously.

Alton bristled and drew himself up to his full height. "Of course I can!"

The clerk passed it off. "Bigger men than you have thought that, too, until they got down into the very belly of the earth. It struck fear in their hearts like nothin' they'd known before. Couldn't take the thought of workin' underground with earth pressin' in on all sides—"

"Listen," Alton interrupted sharply as the idea began to

rattle him, too. "I told you I can do it. I ain't scared of nothin'. Now do you want me or not?"

The clerk looked amused. "Maybe you can at that, stranger. If you're wantin' to learn, we've got the miners who can teach you."

Quickly the clerk explained the routine. He assigned Alton to a vacant shack and jotted down his name and number, making Alton an official employee of the coal mine.

"You can buy what you need at the company store on credit," the clerk went on. "Without a wife and family, Mr. Wheeler, you shouldn't have any trouble stayin' on good terms with the store." The clerk explained the procedures for accounting.

"I've got enough cash, so I don't expect no trouble at the store," Alton said.

"And here's your token," the clerk said, rummaging in a drawer and bringing out a brass disc. He jotted the identification number in a book and beside it penned Alton's name. "Put this token on top of each loaded coal car you send up. When the men dump it, the fellow who keeps records will credit the car to your account and send the marker back down into the shaft for you to have for your next load. You'll be paid by the load, so work fast. But don't try to skimp and short the company."

"I'm not stupid," Alton muttered indignantly. "And I'm no cheat!"

"Don't get your dander up, feller," the clerk said evenly. "I'm paid to give instructions—and that's what I'm doin'. These are your tools." The clerk handed them across the desk. "A pick. Your carbide lamp. Do you think you can remember how to work it?" he asked after demonstrating.

Alton nodded. "I reckon so."

"If you forget, someone can show you. I guess you're ready to start work tomorrow when the whistle blows. Good luck."

Alton grunted a response. The door of the shack banged shut behind him and he returned to the team. He unloaded his gear by the dilapidated shanty, then drove the team from the coal camp and returned to the nearby farm. The farmer came out to meet him, a questioning look on his face when he recognized Alton.

"It's about my horses," Alton began. "You said you could use them, but not me. How much would it be worth to you to have 'em to use as your own until I have need for 'em again?"

The farmer thought a moment, then named a figure. "Plus all the grain and hay they can eat," he added.

"Then it's a deal," Alton said. "And I'll throw in the use of my wagon."

Alton patted Doc and Dan, then hurried down the road and back to the coal camp, secure in the knowledge the Clydesdales would be well cared for.

The next morning Alton was ready to go to work before the whistle shrilled. When he entered the dark tunnel, he experienced scalp-tingling fear. Stepping into the bowels of the earth was as fearsome as the pits of hell described by the itinerant preachers on the streets of St. Louis.

Alton felt immeasurable relief when he rounded a bend and heard the echo of voices bouncing off the tunnel walls. Directly ahead he saw the bobbing, darting glint of carbide lights. At his approach the men turned to welcome the stranger into their midst before resuming their work. Alton soon learned that conversation was limited to the cracking of jokes, the barking of orders, and the cursing of the black coal that resisted the tug of their picks.

Alton was poignantly aware that he was an outsider. The bantering of the miners excluded him, but Alton didn't mind. He knew the tight little band of men who'd worked side by side long months would eventually expand to admit him, just as the close-knit neighbors in Salt Creek accepted him when he proved himself one of them.

He was right. But it took a full month before Alton knew he had at last broken into the inner circle.

As he emerged from the inky darkness of the mine to blink into the fading sunlight one afternoon, one of the miners gripped his shoulder affectionately and wished him a pleasant evening. It was not long before he was receiving regular invitations to supper.

Alton thought of the scores of pals from the saloons with whom he had idled away so many hours. Not one of them had ever invited him home to meet the family. In fact, most of them seemed to be avoiding home altogether. Yet, here in these simple shanties, Alton saw the undisguised love of wives and children for the grime-covered men who trudged home day after weary day. Looking on, he hungered for the contentment he saw mirrored in their faces.

"You *never* married?" a miner's wife murmured one night and shook her head as if the idea seemed ridiculous. When Alton met her eyes, it was like staring into the wise gaze of Fanny Preston.

"Nope. Never did," he said lightly.

"That's a shame." The miner's wife spoke the words as if she believed any woman would be lucky to have a man like Alton for a husband.

"I came close once, though," Alton found himself admitting. "Real close."

The woman's husband laughed, winking at Alton. "Close in

love ain't like close in horseshoes. Close in love don't count for a thing!"

The cluster of people laughed except for the miner's wife. From the soft look in her eyes, Alton sensed she knew the truth, just as Fanchon Preston did.

"Better to come close in love once in your life," she defended, "than go through life never knowin' the miracle of carin' about someone else like you care for yourself. You've got it so good," she suddenly grew playful and turned to her husband, "that you've plumb forgot what it's like to be a man alone!"

"How about playin' us a tune on your harmonica, Al? My woman just made one of those statements where any answer I'd give would be the wrong one!"

At the urging of the others, Alton took out his harmonica, warmed up, then trilled and wavered through several well-known tunes. His songs were light. But both Alton and the miner's wife knew his heart was heavy with the bittersweet memory of one woman's love.

chapter

7

ALTON HAD HIMSELF only recently been accepted into the fraternity of miners when another man was assigned to their party.

It was a warm day in late August when Alton and the other men stopped their work to determine the source of an unfamiliar tread. Profiled against the smudgy walls, poorly visible by the light of the carbide lamps, was a tall, raw-boned young man with a shock of hair the color of ripe wheat. Alton sensed uncertainty in the fair-haired miner. Remembering his own hesitation at broaching the close-knit group, Alton was the first to set aside his pick and welcome the man.

"The name's Alton Wheeler," he said. He offered a beefy grip after swiping the grit and coal dust across the seat of his pants.

"I'm Tom McPherson," the younger man replied in a low, quiet voice. His words were directed to Alton, but his pleasant smile swept the cavern to encompass them all.

"Pleased to meet ya, Tom."

Alton began the introductions. Tom nodded to each man in turn and spoke a few words of greeting.

The men returned to their work. Tom, sensing a special warmth in Alton Wheeler, moved to work alongside him. He studied Alton's routine before adopting it for himself. Gradually conversation sprang up between the two.

"You're not from these parts, are you?" Alton asked. "The reason I ask is you talk sort of funny. With kind of a twang I can't rightly place."

"Kentucky. Paducah, originally, that is," Tom clarified. "I've been livin' in Illinois quite a spell, though. In Fayette County, not far from Vandalia. Sadie—that's my wife—she says she 'spects I'll sound like I do until the day I die."

"Vandalia, eh? I passed through on my way here. Looks like a nice town."

"We live out of town apiece," Tom explained. "About ten miles north."

"You're a ways from Kentucky, boy. How'd you happen into these parts?"

"It's kind of a long story."

"Time's one thing we've got down here," Alton grunted. "Tell me if you want—or keep it to yourself if you don't."

"I've got nothin' to hide," Tom said.

Tom remained silent for so long Alton wondered if the lanky fellow were going to take his suggestion, after all. When he spoke, Alton realized Tom McPherson had merely been organizing his thoughts. Alton listened as Tom provided the few details that added up to his life.

"I drifted for a while after my folks died," Tom said. "Never really found any area completely to my likin' until I worked for a farmer near Vandalia." The tall man laughed softly. "Maybe it was because Sadie lived there that made it seem the nicest place I'd ever settled." Alton chuckled, too. "I married her and made arrangements to buy a farm near her folks' small place."

"If you're a farmer, how come you're workin' the mines?" asked Alton, suddenly interested.

106

"Had a run of misfortune last year," Tom explained, "includin' a poor crop. Minin' seemed the only way to secure the farm. You ever do any farmin'?"

"I've done my share of sod-bustin' . . . some last spring over in Effingham County. A small place on the banks of Salt Creek."

"Then you know what it's like," Tom nodded. "Takes a lot of jack . . . and manpower . . . to keep a place goin'."

"Who's standin' in fer you while you're gone?"

"Sadie and her younger brother Benjamin are workin' the crops and tendin' the young'uns while I save up some money. But bein' away from 'em won't last forever, thank the Lord."

"I 'spect you miss 'em, don't ya?" sympathized Alton.

Tom nodded. "As much as they miss me," he admitted. "It was hard on poor Sadie when I boarded the train. Like to have broke my heart the way she tried to be so brave." Tom gave Alton a faint smile. "It wasn't exactly easy on me, either, leavin' her and the kids."

Alton thought how difficult it had been to leave Sue Ellen, even with his anger to spur him on. "It won't last forever," he echoed vaguely.

"We'll take it one day at a time," Tom said. "Knowin' I've got Sadie to go home to makes being apart easier to take."

"Your Sadie must be quite a woman," Alton said. In Tom, he sensed the same feelings for Sadie that he kept secretly locked away in his heart for Sue Ellen.

There was quiet pride in Tom's eyes when he nodded. "The Lord gave me a good woman when he gave me Sadie. I try to be everything Sadie could want and need in a man. But you know how it is . . . she deserves a better man than I'll ever be."

"No, I don't guess I do know how 'tis," Alton said, cocking his head. "Never had a wife myself." He chinked away at the coal that fell in blue-black fragments to form a pile at his feet.

Tom regarded Alton with fresh curiosity. "You never married?"

"Nope." Alton grimaced and slammed the pick hard.

Tom turned back to his work. "I thought maybe you'd been married. Maybe you'd lost your woman to the sickness. We lost my ma and Sadie's to the cholera three years back. Sadie's pa pined away and was dead within the year."

"Naw. Never married," Alton said. "And I only had the itch to once, but I scratched that itch pretty handily and gave up the idea." He gave a dry laugh.

"Don't you have a sweetheart?"

"Naw. Well . . . I mean, yeah! Sure. Sure I do! I've got a real nice sweetie. Pretty as can be." Alton's pulse quickened just remembering how beautiful Sue Ellen looked that morning following the barn raising.

Alton had never mentioned Sue Ellen to the other miners. In Tom McPherson, though, he sensed a man who would understand. Sadie, it seemed, had given Tom all the joys Alton wished, dreamed, and crudely prayed that he could have found with Sue Ellen.

"What's she like—your sweetheart?" Tom asked.

"Oh, well, now—" Alton screwed up his face in thought. "Let me see. Why, I'd say she's probably a lot like your Sadie." Enough time had passed so Alton took only pleasure and received no pain in remembering. "She's a good woman, Sue Ellen is. A Christian woman . . . and a lady . . . like your Sadie. Sue, she's a fine cook and can sew real fancy. She likes to make quilts. She made me one. She's pleasin' to the eye, too, with her long dark hair—black as a crow's wing and kind of curly. Her eyes are as green as the first blades of grass come March."

"Sounds real nice."

"The nicest gal *I* ever met! I probably would've married Sue

108

Ellen, but she's a widow woman. I didn't feel I could ask her to forget her husband so soon and have me. Although I sure wanted to, mind you. I had Sue's feelin's to consider, you know," Alton fibbed magnanimously.

"Maybe it'll work out yet," Tom suggested. "The time wasn't right then. But that doesn't mean that sometime in the future you won't get a second chance."

It was an idea Alton had not stopped to consider. He halted his work and leaned on his pick, studying Tom's face to detect if he were joshing. He decided quickly the young miner was not.

"You think so, boy?" Alton asked softly. "You believe that?"

Tom glanced at Alton, surprised by the seriousness in his voice. Alton looked as if his very life depended on Tom's truthful answer.

"Sure I do," he replied. "Sometimes God shows us a little glimpse of what He's got in store for us. Then the next thing we know, life comes along and upsets the applecart until it looks like what seemed so perfect at one time couldn't possibly be what the Lord had in mind. We give up on the idea, go on with livin', and after time passes, end up gettin' what we'd one time had our heart set on, but couldn't manage to get no matter how hard we tried on our own."

Alton thought it over. "It's an odd thing, Tom. You even talk kind of like Sue Ellen. I can't rightly say the things she said made a heap of sense to me at the time. But she was so serious and all about how she felt this God had everything lined up neat 'n' orderly for her from the day she first drawed breath to her dyin' moment, that I couldn't poke fun at her. Sue Ellen acted like God had these same kind of plans— purpose, I think she called it—for me. For everybody. I always figgered she was just carryin' on like women tend to do. 'Cause I'm one feller that makes his own decisions!"

Tom chuckled. "A lot of people like to think they do, Alton. But Sue Ellen's right. God's in control of our lives. A lot of us have tried to take the reins away from Him and trick ourselves into thinkin' we're in charge. In the process of tryin' to control our destinies, sometimes we cause ourselves and others a lot of misery. True happiness," Tom said in a voice not much above a whisper, "comes in livin' each day—not for yourself, or even for others, but for the Lord. Real happiness, Alton, is found in doin' the Lord's will. Even when it hurts."

Alton's lip twitched. "You sound like some kind of preacher. Are you?"

"No, I'm not," Tom said. "But I've read the Good Book a lot. I guess I know it well enough to preach, but I don't figure the Lord saw fit for me to be one to stand behind a pulpit. Appears He has better use for me elsewhere."

Alton was relieved. "I couldn't really picture you a preacher, Tom. Most of 'em I've seen have been weak sisters. Never do work any heavier than liftin' a Bible to shake in your face. I must say, you make more sense than some of 'em, too. All I ever heard was threats of hellfire. Never heard 'em talk the way you and Sue Ellen do."

Tom shrugged. "Preachers are human. Sometimes they forget to talk about God's love and forgiveness." A smile curved his lip. "Hellfire and damnation are more apt to get people to sit up an' take notice, I reckon."

"Got a picture of your Sadie?" Alton asked, changing the subject.

"In my shack."

"I'd like to see it sometime," Alton ventured boldly. "An' I'll show you Sue Ellen's picture so you'll know what she looks like."

Alton fell silent and so did Tom. For a while the only sound that could be heard was the steady *chink, chink* of steel against rock as they picked at the stubborn earth.

Alton's thoughts drifted back to the days spent with Sue Ellen. What must have been a million memories played through his mind. That first night when Alton had found the picture of Sue Ellen in the damp grass, he'd tucked it away with his cherished possessions—his mother's locket, the pocket knife that had been his father's, the expensive green ribbon he had bought at the general store in Effingham.

Alton had meant to return the picture to Sue Ellen. He'd put off the action in hopes that, when he offered it to her, she'd tell him he could keep it. A few times since leaving, he'd puzzled over the situation and wondered what she would think if she knew he had taken her picture without permission. He'd found it, sure. But in keeping it, had he stolen it?

What difference did it make, Alton decided brusquely. Once more the last images of Sue Ellen flashed to mind to haunt him. The memory of her running away without a backward glance, as if she couldn't get away fast enough, chilled him to the bone.

Alton attacked the vein of coal with renewed force. Stealing! It was a small thing to worry about. So what if he hadn't asked for her picture? He had it! Sue Ellen hadn't asked for his love, either—but she had it. If he'd stolen Sue Ellen's picture, maybe *she'd* done him even worse. Sue Ellen Stone had stolen his heart.

Late September brought the first days of Indian summer. Alton fell into the daily routine and allowed his thoughts to wander no further than the present.

With his great height, Alton had to stoop to work in the tunnels that wormed beneath the sod, supported by stout

111

wooden beams and sturdy columns of unmined coal that provided some measure of stability. Tom, too, had to bend over, until the ache in their backs became an ever-present reality. Soon they didn't bother to acknowledge or speak of it.

Each morning the men entered the pits, with skin scrubbed as clean as cold water and lye soap would allow. By dusk, they trudged from the shaft stiff, dulled by weariness, and grimy with the gritty black filth of coal dust pressed into every pore.

Most of the miners cursed their fate. Alton grumbled right along with them, but in his heart he looked forward to the hours spent in the tunnel with his new friend. For Tom was the first true friend Alton had ever called his own. Not that Will Preston and the others hadn't been neighborly. It was just that, with Tom McPherson, Alton shared a special kinship, and he refused to consider the day when Tom would return to his wife and family.

Alton knew Tom cherished him, too. In fact, the two men had become almost inseparable, to the amusement of the other miners who couldn't fathom the special bond that linked the coarse, dark-haired, flint-tempered giant to the serene, slow-talking farmer.

On most days Alton and Tom worked a short distance away from the others, giving them some privacy to converse. Alton discovered that, once Tom overcame his initial shyness, the young miner was quite a talker. Warming to his subject, Tom could go on for hours. It was obvious that Tom spoke frankly only to those he truly trusted, and it warmed Alton to know that he was among the select few.

"You know, Preacher Tom," Alton murmured, casting him an assessing glance. "You're kind of an odd 'un. You're the first feller I've met who was religious—*real* religious—but wasn't some kind of sissy."

Tom laughed, and Alton was relieved to see that his friend

took no offense. "Lots of strong men figure they don't need the Lord." Tom winced as the loose coal fragments sprayed his face. "But He makes the weak strong and the strong weak, so that all can realize their need of Him."

"That's another thing, Tom," the big man said, "you talk about this God—the Lord, you call Him—as if you could reach out and touch Him like you could me. Just as if you could invite Him over to play the harmonica when you've a notion to take your banjo down and strum a few chords."

Tom rested on his pick to regard Alton for a moment.

"Yup, I guess I do," he admitted softly. "The Lord *is* real to me, Alton. As real as you are. Even though we can't touch Him or see Him, He's here right now."

Alton glanced around, an eerie feeling raising the hair on the back of his neck. He didn't look convinced, and he hoped Tom couldn't detect the open doubt he suspected was betrayed by his countenance.

"Oh, I know *you* feel that way, Tom. It just struck me as odd that you'd think of Him as a—a best friend, when you can't even see Him, or know what He looks like, or recognize His footsteps, or see the color of His eyes."

"The Lord *is* my Best Friend, Alton. The Lord is the best—and only—friend any of us really need."

"*He's* your best friend?" Alton whispered, and bit his lip. "But I thought—" Alton hit the wall a crushing blow with his pick. He didn't look at Tom again. He couldn't. Alton didn't want to chance that the young miner would see the hurt in his eyes.

Alton's heart burned with the cruel knowledge. For long weeks that had turned into months, he had worked side by side with Tom. In all that time he'd come to believe—had *reason* to believe—that *he* was the younger man's best friend. Land sakes, he'd never felt for another man what he did for

113

Tom. Tom—who didn't get insulted when Alton teasingly called him "preacher." Tom—who was so good, so kind, so decent that Alton actually felt he could die for such a man if he had to. Alton assumed he was Tom's best friend, too, and it stung like the bite of a mud dabber wasp to know *he* wasn't because some invisible, ghostly *God* was!

On the way out of the mine, Alton was uncomfortably aware that Tom was sticking close as they picked their way through the mass of workers shuffling from the shaft. He caught glimpses of Tom mopping his face with his handkerchief, baring a patch of white beneath the gritty coal dust. But when Tom fell in step beside him, Alton stared straight ahead, not even acknowledging the younger man's presence.

"Alton, what's wrong?"

Alton forced a broad smile to mask his feelings and his eyes drifted guiltily from Tom's probing stare. "Nothing," Alton grunted evasively. "Nothin' a'tall."

"You're sure?" Tom asked. "Al, if I said something wrong, I'm sorry. Or, if there's something you want or need to talk about, I'm here. I'm your friend."

"It wasn't nothin' you said, Preacher Tom," Alton lied quickly. "And there ain't nothin' bothering me, neither." Alton avoided Tom's eyes. "I'm just tired. All right?"

"Sure," Tom agreed and quickly managed a smile of his own.

But things weren't all right with Alton.

He felt a dull, burning ache inside. God, *again!* Alton wondered at the strange relationship Tom—and Sue Ellen— had with this Lord of theirs. To listen to them, you wouldn't doubt that He was the joy of their lives. To Alton? Well, this God of theirs had a mighty bad habit of getting in the way! Alton wanted Sue Ellen like he'd never wanted any other woman, and she'd thrown him over for—*God.* When he had dared to believe he was Tom McPherson's best friend, he'd been bluntly informed he was not, and never could be, because Tom's Best Friend was—*God*.

But just as he still loved and longed for Sue Ellen Stone, Alton knew he'd accept Tom McPherson, too, on any terms.

chapter

8

EXCEPT FOR THE one afternoon when he had grown sullen and silently hostile after Tom explained his relationship with the Lord, Alton was his easygoing self. Since that wretched day, Alton had decided it was better to settle for a lesser place in the affections of a man like Tom than not to have a place at all.

Throughout the ensuing days, their friendship grew deeper and stronger. More and more often, Alton found himself entertaining regrets when Tom began to speak in vague terms about returning to his wife and children.

"Are you goin' home for Christmas?" Alton asked.

"No." Tom's answer was startling.

Alton stopped his work and rested his arms on the handle of the pick.

"Why, if that don't beat all!" he blurted. "I was sure you'd take off 'n' go home for Christmas like some of the other fellers, Tom! I figgered you'd go back to Sadie and your young'uns with a bag full of presents like Santy Claus."

"Not this year," Tom said with a rueful smile. Alton knew then how very much Tom would have enjoyed returning home in just the manner described.

"How come you're not goin'?"

"Sadie and I agreed I wouldn't make a trip home till I could go home for good. I'll go for plantin' season—not before. As mild as the weather's been this winter, it might even be earlier this year than last."

"I hate to think of the day when we won't be workin' the tunnels together," Alton admitted reluctantly.

Tom touched Alton's shoulder. "Me, too, Alton. By the way, I didn't think to ask. What are *your* plans for Christmas?"

"I ain't made any."

"Then you're not goin' to be with family or friends?"

"No family to be with. And no friends, either, 'cept—"

"The Stones. They're not close enough to make a trip worthwhile?"

"They're better'n a hundred miles away."

Alton had never bothered to tell Tom that he wasn't sure he'd even be welcome at Sue Ellen's farm any more. He had been satisfied to share only his happy memories with Tom, keeping the miserable ones to himself to brood over in private.

Eventually talk of the coming holiday ceased between the two men, and their conversation drifted to other matters.

On Christmas Eve Alton returned to his shack. That night he went to bed early, huddling beneath Sue Ellen's quilt as a chilly breeze rattled through the clapboards to steal away what warmth he gained when he entertained idle imaginings about Sue Ellen and Jem.

Were they celebrating with Fanny and Will? Had the preacher returned to hold special Christmas services? Maybe they'd be seeing Lizzie and Harmon, too. And the Childerses would have their little one by now. Alton wondered if Lizzie had borne Harm a son or a daughter to be wrapped in the quilt Sue Ellen had sewn with love in every stitch.

The mine was closed on Christmas Day. Knowing he was free of duties for the day, Alton slept dreamlessly.

He was hovering somewhere between deep sleep and moments of fleeting wakefulness when a battering on his cabin door rattled it on its hinges, jerking him wide awake. He bolted upright in bed and threw aside the quilt. The door rattled again.

"Who's there?"

"It's Tom," came the reply. "Open up!"

"Come on in, Tom," Alton invited, reaching for his clothes. "The door's unlatched."

Alton buttoned his shirt, shivering with the blast of frigid air that accompanied Tom inside.

When the ashes in the small coal stove glowed low, Alton stirred the fire and dumped coal from the bucket into the stove. He rubbed his hands together to ease the chill, pretending deep preoccupation with the fire so as not to notice the package Tom was carrying.

But the package, wrapped in white tissue paper and tied clumsily with a garish ribbon, was difficult to overlook.

"For you, Alton. Merry Christmas!"

"Fer me?" There was no need to pretend amazement.

Alton reached for the package, then yanked his hand back and shook his head. He stared in at the glowing coal before he banged the stove door shut and faced Tom.

"I ain't got nothin' fer you, Preacher Tom," Alton explained with embarrassment. "So I can't take it. Won't."

Tom forced the package on him. "That doesn't matter, Alton. I want you to have this gift. In fact, I've been meanin' to give it to you ever since I came. On a whim I decided to wait until Christmas, thinkin' receivin' it as a present now might make it more special somehow."

"What is it?" Alton asked in an almost wary tone as he accepted the surprisingly solid package.

With a mischievous smile, Tom winked. "Open it and find out!"

With a quick glance, almost as if asking Tom's permission, Alton began shredding the paper. He couldn't remember the last time someone had given him a gift. Sue Ellen's quilt had been a spontaneous gesture with no wrapping to hide the treasure. Besides, the more he pondered it, Sue Ellen had acted more like the quilt was payment owed than an outright gift given in friendship—or love.

The paper fell away to reveal the contents. A book! Alton spelled out the title. H–O–L–Y B–I–B–L–E.

"It's right thoughtful of ya." Alton forced a hearty tone. "Never had a Bible before. Tom, you shouldn't have."

Alton hoped Tom couldn't detect the nameless disappointment he suffered at discovering the contents of the package.

"Yes, I should," Tom corrected. "Sadie squirrels away pennies and then buys up new Bibles every chance she gets. She packed that one in with my own and told me that when I met a soul in need of it, I'd know, and to make him a gift of the Good Book. I knew it was goin' to be yours almost as soon as we met, Alton. I was just waitin' for the right time to give it to you."

"Well, thanks, Tom, and you thank Sadie for me, too," Alton said. "I have to warn you, though. I can read—but not very good." He paused, realizing how ungrateful he sounded. "But I'll tell you what, Tom, I'll sure give it a try. It ain't every day I get a gift."

Tom nodded, smiling. "The gift of the book, Alton, that's from Sadie and me. But the gift of understandin' . . . now that'll come from the Lord. I'll be prayin' that He'll favor you with the knowledge He wants you to have."

Not quite knowing what to say, Alton turned away and carefully placed the black leather book on the makeshift table beside his bed.

"Do you read the Bible much, Tom?"

Tom nodded. "Every mornin'. Today it was the story of the Virgin Birth. Here, I'll find it for you, Alton," he offered. "I'll leave the page marked so you can read about the Lord's birth yourself if you've a mind to."

Tom fanned through the pages and inserted a marker before he closed the book and handed it back to Alton.

"Preacher Tom," Alton stared at his feet, shuffling with discomfort. "I-I've got to tell you somethin'."

"What is it?"

Alton's deep voice shook. He could scarcely speak above a whisper. "You'll never know how dreadful sorry I am I don't have a gift for you. After you bein' so good to me 'n' all. I guess it just goes to show how selfish I am. . . ." His voice trailed away.

"Alton," Tom said. "I *told* you that doesn't matter."

"It does to me," Alton said quietly. "I knew it was Christmas, Tom. You've been like family to me. I could've got you a little somethin'. You, Tom, away from your wife and young'uns. You, who ain't used to spendin' Christmas alone. Not like I am anyway—"

Tom smiled shyly. "I was kind of countin' on you giving me somethin', Alton. Maybe you don't have anything wrapped up, but I was settin' great store that you'd make me a gift of your time. I was hopin' we could spend the day together."

"That's worth somethin' to you?" Alton murmured.

"It's worth more than you'll ever know, friend."

"Well, then, Tom," Alton said and swelled with a pleasant sense of importance, "let's make this a day to remember.

'Stead of feelin' sad and out of sorts, you get your banjo, I'll get my harmonica, and I'll bet there's others in this coal camp who'd like an excuse to make merry. This'll be a day to remember!"

"The Lord would like that," Tom said.

"He would?" Alton cocked his head and stared, mystified.

"He sure would!"

Sometimes it amazed Alton the way Tom could talk about the Lord—as if He were a fellow Tom knew well. As if he knew for sure the Lord loved banjo pickin' and harmonicas.

Maybe the Lord did enjoy things the way other people did, Alton mused. Now that he had a Bible of his own, he planned to find out. Reading wouldn't be easy, but Alton figured he could do it. Maybe then, he'd come to know this Lord Tom found so wonderful. Maybe if he read the words for himself, he'd even come to understand the Lord's ways. Like Tom did. And like Sue Ellen—

Just as Tom had predicted, the winter was a mild one. Warm days were broken by short-lived cold snaps. Twice, blizzards raged, howling over the land and piling snowdrifts at angles. Then the sun would come out, warm and bright, and burn away the evidence as the snow melted to puddles beneath the blue skies.

"You were right, Preacher Tom, about the season bein' an easy one."

"Suspected it might be," Tom said. "The coat of the woolyworm gave me a clue. Then the buzzards stayed around instead of flyin' south. And the horses' coats were light this year. If a harsh season had been in store, nature's signs would've foretold it."

"You'll be able to start farmin' early this year, I'll bet."

"I might at that, though I don't pretend to know what the Good Lord has in store. I hope to head home come April."

"I'm goin' to miss you, boy." Alton's voice became tight.

"I'll miss you, too, and feel hurt if you don't make plans to come visit Sadie and me. Everyone in Vandalia knows where we live. Findin' us would be easy."

"Might do that sometime," Alton grunted.

"Sadie'd like that. In her letters she writes she's already heard so much about you she considers you kin. And you've no doubt listened to me talk so much about her, you'd recognize Sadie on the street."

"Her—Thad, Amanda Jane, and Katie, too," Alton agreed.

"Then you'll come stay with us sometime?"

Alton thought it over. "Sure I will. If I ever make it down your way, you can reckon on seein' me!"

At the tail end of January, a blizzard raged through the area, followed by southern breezes that warmed the land. Old-timers predicted an early spring, even while they warned of surprise snowstorms that could blow in to remind everyone it was still wintertime.

But they were wrong.

By February the weather was unseasonably warm. Flies buzzed about, and with the arrival of the flies came drizzling rain. The prospect of pneumonia gave way to the specter of cholera that had already broken out in the state.

Cholera!

The word struck fear in every heart.

Everyone knew the symptoms: violent, draining sickness, followed by wracking spasms, then death, hasty burial, and the grim fear of recurring outbreaks.

Alton, like the others, spoke of cholera in a hushed voice as if speaking in a whisper would prevent its arrival in the area. But the dread disease ran rampant.

123

Almost every day telegrams arrived in the coal camp, bringing fearful news from home. Wives. Children. Parents. All taken by the plague. Strong men, stunned by the news, whimpered and broke down, wailing their grief.

Fear clenched Alton's heart in an icy grip when he overheard some of the miners speak of the outbreak in the town near Tom's farm. Alton didn't mention it to his young friend. He sensed Tom already knew, and if he didn't, Alton had no desire to be the one to bring the bad news to his attention.

Three weeks later, after talk of the sickness had begun to die down, Alton entered the shaft and made his way to the place where a cluster of workers in his group gathered to prepare for the day's work. The men spoke in hushed tones, glancing occasionally toward Tom McPherson who stood by himself a short distance from the others—a solitary figure, marked only by the glow from his carbide lamp.

The whispers of the men and Tom's lonely, dejected stance spoke volumes. Alton knew instantly that something had happened. Something tragic.

No one offered to explain. Instead they watched, sober and stricken, as Alton wedged his way past. Stiffly silent, they fell to their work.

Alton halted beside his friend. When the miner looked up, his face was pinched and drawn with grief. Alton stared, shocked at the change in him.

"You've heard?" Tom asked in the face of Alton's silence.

"Heard what?" The words struggled past numb lips.

Tom stared at his feet. His shoulders sagged forward. Then he sucked in his breath, closing his eyes against what seemed almost mortal pain.

"Mandy's dead, Alton," Tom spoke quietly. "Cholera."

"What?" Alton cried. "Oh, God in heaven, no! Tom—*no!*"

"I got the telegram last night."

Alton's eyes brimmed with hot tears. He stared at Tom, unable to comprehend. "Your little girl, Tom?" Alton's voice cracked. "Dead? Last night you knew of it?" Alton was dazed. "Tom, you should have come to me, boy! You didn't have to be alone with your sorrow."

Tom continued to work. "I couldn't stand to be with anyone when I first got the news, Al. But I wasn't alone. The Lord was with me."

There was little Alton could say—so he said nothing.

Stretching torturously between the two men was the silence, broken only by the steady *chunk-chunk* of their picks against the rock walls and the rattle of coal into buckets to be emptied into the carts, shoved up the tracks, and hauled from the pit by mules.

By afternoon Alton had thought the situation through. Angry confusion roiled in his mind until the hot words frothed from his lips. Alton cursed with such violence that Tom stared at him in horror and saw that Alton's eyes were sparking with raw fury.

"That's the most spiteful thing I've seen in all my natural-born days!" Alton cursed again and threw down his pick in a fit of rage. He glared at Tom with such anger that the younger man stopped his work to stare.

"What are you talkin' about, Alton?" Tom asked quietly. "If you said something to me, I'm sorry, but I missed it."

"I wasn't talkin' about *you*, Tom," Alton sputtered. "I was talkin' about that—that God of yours! You may not see it clear, boy, but I sure do. And that God of yours just done you a heap of dirt! What've you ever done to Him? Good, that's what! You tried to live by His ways. If ever I've known a godly man, Preacher Tom, you're it! You've been decent, fair, and righteous like you say folks should try to be. I've never heard you say a mean word about anyone. You've done everything this God of yours wants you to, and what does He do in return? Pays back your good behavior by doin' you dirt, Tom. That's what!"

Tom's mouth dropped open. Stunned, he shook his head. But Alton rushed on, mindful of nothing but this seeming injustice and his need to vent his rage.

"Alton, don't talk like that!" Tom managed to break in. "You don't know what you're sayin'!"

Alton spat on the ground. "'Course I do! I can see it plain as day. You're the one with the foggy notions, Tom! I'm surprised you ain't mad as blue blazes. You've been double-crossed, boy. Maybe you ain't het up about it, but I sure as the devil am!"

"Maybe that's how you see it, Alton. I can't fault you for your feelin's. But that's not how it is for me. Sure, Alton," Tom admitted softly, "I hurt. I feel as if part of my heart has been torn right out. I'm so numb with sorrow I can hardly think. But I know one thing, and one thing only—God loves me, and God loves my little Mandy. God gave Mandy to Sadie and me to love for as long as He wanted us to have her. Mandy was our baby—but she was God's child, too. The Lord had the right to call her home. I'd be lyin' to you if I said it didn't hurt. But I don't question the Lord. Instead I have to thank Him for lettin' us have Amanda Jane to brighten our lives for as long as she did."

Tom fell silent and Alton hadn't the heart to challenge the stricken young miner.

"You would think like that," Alton said gruffly and gave Tom a gentle look. "You're goin' home . . . ain't ya?"

"No," Tom said dully. "There's nothin' I can do for Mandy.

As scared as everyone is of cholera, they buried her immediately."

"There may be nothin' you can do for your little 'un, Tom, but I was kind of thinkin' about your woman. Poor Sadie must be needin' you somethin' awful."

"I'm sure she does. But she's got One Who's stronger than I am."

"I don't care!" Alton flared. "*You* need to be home with your woman, Tommy. She needs *you*. And whether you admit it or not, you stubborn young sprout, you need her, too."

"I'm not denyin' it, Al," Tom said. "I'd love nothing more than to go home to Sadie, but in the telegram she told me there was no use to miss work. Wouldn't bring Mandy back. Besides, it won't be very long before I hope to leave for good. Sadie said to stay on and earn money for the farm."

Alton cursed the money. Gradually his jumbled thoughts untangled and he saw a clear course before him.

"I recognize that look on your face, Alton Wheeler, you big lout," Tom warned in an affectionate drawl. "Don't you dare take off that filthy hat of yours 'n' pass it amongst the men. The fellers need their money for their own families. You give up that idea right now ... 'cause I won't allow it!"

"It was only a thought," Alton lied with an injured air. Quickly he turned away from Tom so he couldn't search his face further and discover the real truth.

"Well, forget it," Tom repeated. "Thanks for the kind thought. But the Lord will take care of me 'n' mine, Alton. He'll give us strength to make it through whatever we have to face. God will provide. He always has."

Alton could only shake his head in wonder. Two of a kind they were—Tom McPherson and Alton's sweet Sue Ellen.

chapter
9

ALTON STRETCHED. He was bent and stiff from a brutal day in the mine and mentally exhausted from wrestling with the confusing emotions that Tom's predicament had spawned in him.

When Tom trudged wearily toward his shack and was safely out of sight, Alton quickened his steps and rushed to his own shanty. He washed off the worst of the grime, tossed the basin of brackish water into the yard, put on a clean shirt, and raked his hair into place.

Then he took some of the pay he'd squirreled back for small purchases from the knotted sock beneath his mattress. He cursed his luck at having put the biggest chunk of his wages into the nearby bank so it would be there, safe, when he needed it. Well, he needed it now, but he hadn't reckoned on banking hours, weekends, or the strange set of circumstances that hindered him from getting his money on time.

Alton stuffed the few greenbacks he had into his pocket and slipped from his shack. Cutting across the muddy field, he ignored the fact that the soles of his boots were becoming heavy and clogged with cold mud.

Doc and Dan recognized him and crossed the pasture to meet him.

"Hello, babies," Alton crooned to the massive horses and stroked their thick necks. "I've come to borrow you boys back fer a little while."

Approaching the farmhouse, he banged on the door. When the woman answered and summoned her husband, Alton made short work of stating his problem. At the farmer's nod, the big man smiled for the first time.

"The horses will be back come mornin'," Alton promised.

Doc and Dan stood quietly while Alton piled on the harness, cursing the time it took to buckle and fasten all the straps and hitches. Finally he was ready to go. The wagon wheels creaked and groaned down the road, but the horses, eager to run, hurried toward the glow of lights from a nearby town.

Alton halted the team in front of a saloon. Laughter spilled into the street as he swung the door wide open. The tinny sound of a piano contrasted with the silent night. An owl hooted in the distance. Alton shivered, and pushed his way into the warm tavern.

The saloon girl gave him a glance and decided he was too shabby, too unkempt, and too poor for her attention. She turned to widen her smile for a nattily dressed young man who entered on Alton's heels.

The short, swarthy barkeep, his shirt rolled past his elbows, cocked a brow at Alton. "Come on in, fella. Have a drink."

"Not right now," Alton refused and walked on.

For what he had in mind, Alton knew he needed his wits about him. He had to find some money for Tom and Sadie—and fast! Maybe God would provide, just as Tom said, but if that were the case, then He was taking His sweet time about it. Alton reasoned that, if he didn't take matters into his own hands—and soon—it'd be too late by the time God got around to it.

Alton sauntered over to watch the poker game in progress. Haunted by Sue Ellen's warnings about such things, he wavered, but the decision seemed made for him when he was invited into the game.

Alton felt as if luck had just lit upon him. Gingerly he accepted the warm chair. He was going to provide for Tom McPherson! And, if luck was with him—provide well! Surely, Sue Ellen—and even Tom himself—wouldn't be too upset over a few hands of cards.

Or would they?

Alton frowned and tried to recall what it was Sue had said once—something to the effect that it wasn't right to do evil in hope that good would eventually come of it.

"Are you in or not?" the dealer asked with sharp impatience, jolting Alton from his memories.

"Oh. Sure. Sure I'm in," Alton said, picking up his cards.

"Then ante up, bumpkin!" snapped the dealer, who'd been losing heavily.

Alton bristled, resisting the urge to reach across the table and shake his fist under the nose of the surly little man. Hmph! He acted as if he, Alton Wheeler, didn't even know how to play the game.

Then the idea came to him. Though Alton's face revealed nothing, deep inside he was grinning.

Slumping in his chair, Alton scratched his head and feigned a look of confusion. He pretended not to notice the others' amusement as he fussed with his cards, clutching them tightly in his fingers.

Let them think I'm a simpleton, he thought. *Let them take me for a fool.* He'd gladly go along with the charade if it meant he'd win enough money to put Tommy on the train home come morning.

131

With the instincts of a fox, Alton played the first hand poorly, bidding wildly, cursing his luck when he lost.

A player sitting across from him twisted the gold rings on his fingers. While he waited for Alton to proceed, the man's pale eyes glittered and a faint smile curved his lips as he bit down on his thin, expensive cigar.

"Your deal, stranger," a player said and snapped the deck of cards onto the table in front of Alton.

With a humble, almost apologetic grin, Alton accepted the deck. His dark brows dipped in a furrow of concentration. Studiously he tried to mimic the others and shuffle the cards with an exhibition of flair. Instead, the cards sprayed into the air and rained in disorder onto the table. Muttering and groaning apologies, Alton clumsily patted the cards into a heap, smashed them together, and began anew with little more success.

After a third attempt, he looked up to see if his efforts had been considered sufficient. They had. Clenching the deck, jerking the cards off the top, Alton dealt. Crudely. Irritatingly slowly.

"How many cards do you get?" he asked.

The cigar-chomper gave him a withering look. "Being as we're playing five-card draw—five, you simpleton!"

"Right. Right," Alton grunted and gave the man an embarrassed grin. He slapped an additional card in front of each player, then set the deck down, and picked up his own hand. The other players gracefully fanned their cards while Alton wrestled and shoved his own into some semblance of order.

"I'll take two." Tapping his cigar ash, the player discarded cards and waited for Alton to deal him fresh ones. On around the table it went.

"Who'll open?"

Squinting through smoke, the well-dressed man flicked his cards together and fanned them expertly.

"I will," offered another in a bored tone and flipped his bid to the pile of coins in the center of the table.

"What're you opening on?"

"Guts 'n' stupidity," joked the man.

The other players made their bids solemnly.

"What's your bid?" They regarded Alton.

"Oh! It's my turn?" he asked absentmindedly and studied the cards with a frown. "I—I don't know what to bid. I lost so much last time, though, I'd better try to win it back before I go home." Alton laid his cards face down on the table and searched his pockets for change before he took out the roll of money—a few greenbacks wrapped around a wad of plain paper to fatten the roll.

"Can I bid a fiver?"

"Sure."

"Oh, land sakes but I'd better win!" Alton fretted when he placed the bill on top of the pile. "My woman will draw 'n' quarter me iffen she finds out about this!"

"I'll see your five and raise two."

"What do you mean?" Alton asked, narrowing his eyes with suspicion.

"If you want to stay in the game, you've got to shell out more jack, Bub," a player yawned as he explained. "He must think his hand's better'n yours."

"Oh."

Alton gave his cards an agonized look and favored the money in his hand with an equally miserable stare. He counted ticks on the grandfather clock.

"Are you stayin' in or not?" a player nudged impatiently.

"Stayin' in."

Alton hung in, accepting the upped bids until the others eventually folded. The pot was his.

"What'd you have, farmer?" asked the rich man who had stayed in the game to the bitter end.

"You don't have to show him, mate," another player cautioned. "He didn't pay to see."

"Oh, I ain't got nothin' to hide!" Alton assured in a trusting voice. He extended his cards with an eager-to-please grin.

It was an ace-high hand—nothing more. The men at the table groaned. The way Alton had bet, they'd dropped out one by one, positive he held a royal flush.

"Your deal!" the cigar smoker said.

Another man shuffled the cards with finesse and dealt them with a graceful flourish. Alton clumsily tucked his cards into his large palm. His face held a look of ignorant confusion, but his heart beat wildly with each fresh card. Maybe the Lord *was* providing for Preacher Tom! Land sakes, he'd never seen such a hand!

The bidding began.

Alton parted with each dollar as if it caused him mortal pain. Each time he expressed the worry that he couldn't lose again or he'd have some tall explaining to do when he got home. The men, winking furtively, raised every bet Alton made. Even so, Alton refused to fold.

"I'll check."

"Fold."

"Fold."

"I fold, too."

"I've got trip tens and a pair of bulls for a full house," the cigar chomper said, confident of victory.

Alton frowned. "Well, now, I ain't rightly sure *what* I've got, but I know one thing, I've sure got a passel of spades.

Every card is black as midnight and numbered one after the other like a litter of pups. Does that mean anythin'?"

They all groaned.

"The pot's yours," the rich man murmured. "A straight flush wins."

Alton looked at his pocket watch before he raked the money toward him. "This here game's kind of fun, ain't it?" he said.

He gave the watch another look. "But I'd better hie myself on home afore my woman raises seven kinds of trouble."

Alton expected the usual complaints that it wasn't fair to quit after winning. The players said nothing. He glanced into the back bar mirror and knew why. With his unkempt beard, rough clothing, and work-hardened build, he looked capable of snapping a man in two.

Jamming the money into his pockets, Alton strode from the saloon. The horses, catching his scent, nickered. Their steamy breath drifted in the night air. Alton unwrapped the reins from the brake lever. The horses trotted briskly back to the farm and Alton hurried across the slick, muddy fields to the coal camp. He crawled into bed and closed his eyes, but Alton scarcely slept for picturing Tom's face when he told him he'd be going home.

The morning light was pale in the sky and the sun just peeping over the eastern horizon when Alton threw on his clothes and hurried down the quiet path to beat on Tom's door.

Sleepily the young miner came to the door, clad only in long johns.

"Hurry up, Tom! Get your clothes on," Alton urged.

"What for? What are you talking about?"

"Get packed, boy!"

Tom stopped, his faded overalls in his hand. "Packed? I'm not going anywhere but down in the mine."

Alton beamed. "That's what you think!" he said. "Tom, today you're goin' home to Sadie!"

Tom cocked his head as if there'd been a joke but somehow he had missed the punch line. "Home?" He tasted the word as if it were a treat he dared not savor.

"And don't argue with me!" Alton ordered in a belligerent voice that denied defiance, even though Tom was too stunned to speak. Alton stuffed the money from his pocket into Tom's. "Here's money for the train 'n' other expenses. There's enough to see you back to the mine, too, if you've a notion to return. Or, it'll help tide you over into summer if you stay on the farm."

Tom stared at the money, then at Alton. "Where'd you get this?"

Alton pulled himself up to his full height. He thrust out his chin. "Now just what's that to you?! It's my money 'n' I can give it to you if I want. Givin' it to you, I am, and expectin' you'll not rag me about it! Take it . . . and make me no more neverminds."

"What'd you do? Rob a bank?" Tom joked weakly.

"Now, Preacher Tom, you know me. Would I do somethin' like that?"

Tom grinned and shook his head. "No. You're an ornery cuss, Alton, but not an evil one. I—I . . . thanks. I appreciate the kind thought, but you've worked too hard and long in the mine for this money to push your savings off on me."

Alton realized Tom had no intention of accepting his gift, and he felt exasperated after the night he'd spent earning the money.

"You not only can take it, *you will!*" Alton thundered. "I may have ten years of age on you, boy, but I've got about six inches and fifty pounds, too! If need be, Preacher Tom, I can pick you up like a piece of kindlin', hog-tie you, and throw you on the first train east myself, with orders for you not to be untied 'til the train stops in Vandalia!"

Tom chuckled. "I believe you'd really do it."

"Try me," Alton warned gruffly. "I don't have a family to spend my money on, Tom. You're like kin to me, so don't deny me the pleasure and peace of mind of helpin' you out. Be on the train this mornin' . . . you hear?"

Tom stared at Alton a long moment, then touched Alton's bulging biceps and blinked back tears.

"I will, Alton. I promise . . . 'n' thanks." A grin lit Tom's plain features. "I'll never forget this kindness, and I hope someday to be able to repay you, but if I can't, surely the Lord in His mercy will."

"Well now, that's more like it." A look of relief crossed the big man's face before changing to one of grim speculation. "Are you goin' home for good?" At the idea of not seeing Tom for a long time, maybe never again, Alton was amazed to find a dry lump solidly lodged in his throat and hot tears scalding his eyes.

"Oh, I'll be back. At least to get my gear."

"I'll be hopin' for your return, Tommy. But don't worry 'bout a thing."

"Take care, friend. Lord willin', we'll meet again."

Nodding because he was too choked up to speak, Alton left for the mine as Tom gathered up his meager belongings and prepared to catch the train.

That morning—and for many mornings following—Alton reported for work, feeling as if a part of him were missing. With Tom, he had discovered a natural rhythm that allowed the two to talk while their picks fell in unison, their words crowding away the silence and isolation of the black pit.

The other miners liked him, that Alton knew, but it wasn't the same. They were nice, pleasant, and he enjoyed visiting in their homes again—but there was a difference between a friend and a brother—and Tom McPherson had become more like a brother to Alton.

Days, then weeks slipped by. Alton longed for Tom's return. With spring just around the corner now, he began to wonder if the young miner had decided not to come for his belongings.

The advent of spring brought sluicing downpours that turned the coal camp into a sea of mud. It was almost a relief for the men to leave the pattering rain above ground to descend into the quiet mine.

"They say age before beauty, old-timer!" a youthful miner teased, giving Alton an impish smile. "What do you say you take the mules up with the coal cars this time, and I'll go next? You look like you could use a rest."

Alton spat. "What're you hopin', you sassy pup? That I get kicked in the head? That I get killed by a stubborn, flea-bitten mule like happened to that fellow the other week?"

Alton's rough accusation caused the grin to fade from the youth's features.

"Don't be so touchy," the youngster muttered in a pained voice, his friendly banter giving way to injured indignation. "I was only tryin' to be thoughty. I can see why no one bothers with you! I should've knowed better. Try to be friendly—'n' you bite a fella's head off!" The slight youth turned away, his thin shoulders humping with each angry breath.

"Hey, boy!" Alton called after him. "Ferget I said it. Didn't mean to get so sore, all right? I'm sorry!"

The young man didn't answer, couldn't hear. He was already rounding the next bend in the tunnel.

"I *said* I was sorry!" Alton's words echoed, but there was no answer.

Clucking to the mule, Alton promised himself that somehow he'd make it up to the young fellow. He'd seek him out later, talk with him, prove there were no hard feelings.

Alton grasped the mule's bridle. Tugging hard, he yanked the balky animal up the incline. With each step, the coal cars snapped as they lurched ahead until the last car in line was in motion.

When Alton reached the now-sunlit opening, he had to shield his eyes against the brilliant glare. Then he stood by, speaking reassuringly to the mule while the coal cars were emptied. The mule twitched his long ears back and forth, but his eyes remained half-closed and his hind leg was crooked into a resting position.

"Here you go, fella!" a worker said. Alton held out his hands and the brass tokens clattered into the palm of his hand. He shoved them into his pocket and jerked the mule ahead, turning back to the shaft to begin the descent into the pit.

With each step into the shaft, Alton sensed that something was amiss, although the unusual sound he was hearing wasn't something he could identify. The mule, too, seemed skittish, cocking his ears. Minutes later, Alton rounded a bend in the tunnel. It was then he knew the origin of the swishing noise.

Rushing water!

"Water?" Alton whispered, confused, before the meaning dawned. "Oh, God, *no!*"

The mule, shoved ahead by the rolling empty cars, couldn't halt though Alton gave a powerful yank on the lead rein. His carbide light cast a golden path like that of a miniature moon on the water gurgling higher and higher as it rose in the tunnel.

"No, no, no . . . *no!*"

The word was a horrified chant on Alton's tongue. The water touched his boots. Shocked into action, he jerked at the mule's harness buckles. Water gushed to his ankles. The mule reared. Alton wrestled to free the animal, but the bucking mule resisted his attempts. Finally the buckles worked free. With a bay of terror, the beast snorted, bolted, and knocked Alton aside. The mule's hooves thudded in the dark tunnel, and the carts clattered ahead, then sank into the watery pit with a gurgle of finality.

Alton cupped his hands around his mouth and yelled. His words, absorbed by the approaching water, echoed back hollowly. There was no sound but the wet slosh of the water rising in the pit.

Instincts dictated that Alton should run—run for his life. Helplessly he glanced down at the watery hole. At that moment the limp, lifeless body of the young man who'd only minutes before walked away with an injured air, floated by. His staring eyes were stark and glassy. Alton started to sob. He grabbed for the boy, but his body bobbed just out of reach.

"I'm sorry," Alton whimpered, crying. "Oh, dear God, I'm sorry. So sorry, so sorry—"

The runaway mule alerted those above ground to trouble in the pit. Disturbed by the unidentified commotion, the miners met Alton in the tunnel. From his terrified expression they could only imagine the scene below and waited in mute fear for him to speak.

"They're dead. All of 'em!" Alton sobbed. "Drowned like rats, they were!" His shoulders heaved. "They're dead and by all rights, I should be, too! I should've died in place of that young feller in there. It should've been me." His anguish was overwhelming as he thrashed about, tears streaming down his face.

"Get a grip on yourself, man," ordered a short, stocky miner, giving Alton a gentle shake. "Take it easy now. Calm down." He glanced around, wondering how many strong men it would take to control the big man if he went berserk.

When they led Alton from the tunnel, he was docile, answering their questions as if he had no will of his own. Upon command, Alton produced the tokens from his pocket—the recent dead neatly numbered. They had only to check their records for identification.

"What happened?" asked a mine official.

"Don't rightly know," said Alton. "I swear I don't. Things was normal in the tunnel when I come up with the coal. When I went back, there was water everywhere."

The mining officials reckoned that the ground was wet, soggier than usual, following the relentless rain. In addition, miners had been working perilously close to an underground stream. The bite of a pick had caused a seep. Then a trickle. Suddenly, a gushing torrent to ensnare them all.

"It should've been me," Alton murmured again and again as he stared into the foggy tin mirror in his shanty. "Why couldn't it have been me instead of someone with a wife and children, or a boy with all his life stretched out ahead of him?" Numb, Alton sank to his bed and leaned ahead to nestle his face in his gritty hands. "Oh, God, why couldn't it have been me?"

In his heart, Alton knew why. Just as Preacher Tom knew. As Sue Ellen would know. They'd always said there was a time for everything. A time to be born and a time to die. And it had not been his time to die. Because God meant for Alton Wheeler to live.

chapter
10

ALTON COULDN'T bring himself to enter the mine the next day. Every time he thought of the tunnels worming in all directions beneath the short, scruffy grass that was greening with spring, a dull, aching fear spread in his stomach.

He professed a bellyache. The men nodded, awkwardly patted his shoulder, and assured him he'd feel better the next day. For all their carefully casual manner, Alton suspected they recognized the truth. The fear was relentless, gnawing at him without mercy.

Standing in his crude shack, Alton watched the men trooping to the mines. As the lone survivor of the recent cave-in, Alton would be reassigned to another area. The flooded tunnel would never again be worked.

Back and forth, back and forth, Alton paced the floor. The planks creaked beneath his weight. Somehow the day passed, but that night, sleep eluded him. No matter how tightly he pinched his eyes shut, he saw the boy—grinning, trying to make a joke—before he passed from life to death and floated by in Alton's imagination.

The following morning Alton did not report to the mine. Nor could he force himself to appear the day after. Or the day that followed it.

The men had just left for the tunnels when he heard the sound of footsteps on his path. A sharp rap rattled the door. Probably a mine official ordering him to get back to work, or, more likely, to pack and leave. Alton tried to collect his thoughts.

The door shook again before he could cross the room and yank it open, expecting to find a grim-faced boss. Instead, Tom McPherson leaned against the door frame.

"Tommy! Is it really you?" Alton cried.

Not waiting for the thin man to answer, Alton grabbed him in a bear hug. Tom returned the affectionate embrace, then held Alton at arm's length to study his face.

"It's wonderful to see you, Al."

"And you, too, Preacher Tom!" Alton said, smiling for the first time in days. "I had it figgered you weren't coming back."

"The weather brought me back. Spring's comin' early, just as I thought. But the rain!" Tom shook his head grimly. "It must be like it was in the days when Noah built his ark. It's too wet to think of workin' the fields, so I decided to come to the mine for a few more weeks."

"That's only about as long as I plan to work myself. I've been thinkin' of leavin', Tom, but I can't. Not yet. I've got to go down in the tunnels again. Got to conquer my fear." He paused, searching Tom's face. "You heard 'bout the accident?"

Tom nodded. "They told me no one survived but you. It was the hand of God that saved you, Alton."

"I know."

Alton didn't really know, but the thought *had* occurred to him more than once.

"God spared you for a reason, Alton."

Alton avoided Tom's eyes. He felt vulnerable. But there were some things that needed saying, some stirrings of the soul that he couldn't voice to any other man but Tom McPherson.

"I've been givin' some thought to the things you said, Tom. It's plumb scary." Alton faced his friend squarely. "But for a quirk of fate, I'd have drowned like the rest of 'em."

"It wasn't anything as whimsical as luck or fate. It was God's will, Alton. You were where you were—safe from harm—because the Lord wanted you there. He's got a purpose for your life, Alton, and He has a reason for you to live."

"Mebbe," Alton conceded.

"Are you goin' to work?" In answer Alton shrugged and Tom continued, "I came by to see if you felt up to reportin'. Thought maybe they'd assign us together."

Alton managed a smile. "I—I'd like that. It'd be easier for me, Tom, facin' that black tunnel with you by my side."

"I know," Tom said. "But even if I wasn't here to face it with you, there's One who would be. He's with you, Alton, even when you don't realize it. He's here . . . and He always will be."

"How can you be so sure?" Alton started to say, but he swallowed the words. Such a question would be an open admission that he hadn't read the Bible Tom had given him. He'd tried a time or two. But the words came hard and the way was slow.

As Alton readied himself for the mine, he glanced at the closed Bible. A powdery layer of dust covered it. Alton vowed that if he and Tom entered the mine and came out alive, he'd begin reading that Bible right away, and he'd see his way through a whole chapter before he went to sleep even if it took him half the night. If he could only read as well as Sue Ellen—the words rolled from her tongue smooth as silk. At the thought of her, his pulse quickened.

145

"Ready to leave, Al?"

The big man tensed. He nodded. He slung his pick over his shoulder, the carbide lamp dangling at his side. "Let's go."

Alton made small talk to bolster his courage. Tom listened in silence.

"Take it easy now, Alton," he cautioned.

The two men adjusted their headlamps and stepped into the tunnel. The lights cast eerie, dancing shadows over the rough walls.

"Remember what I said. Nothin' . . . no one can disturb a hair of your head unless the Good Lord lets it happen. And if He allows it, no amount of fear or worry can change anything. The Lord's in control, so we may as well not think fearful thoughts, eh?"

"Right," Alton agreed in a faint tone, trailing behind Tom. Tom, scrutinizing the tunnels, slowed and took a turn. "This must be where the fellers told us to go."

"Must be," Alton agreed. "They probably abandoned this old tunnel when they struck richer veins elsewhere."

"I'll wager it would have gone unmined if not for the accident," Tom surmised.

Alton stiffened at the mention, then bent to his pick with a vengeance. Moments passed before either of the men spoke again.

"Sure is noisy here," Tom observed.

"Ain't it, though?" agreed Alton, relieved that Tom also noticed the subtle creaks and groans that he had half-feared were dark torments rising from his imagination to torture him. "It's enough to give a man a fright."

Tom chuckled. "I thought it was kind of a friendly sound, myself, but it does make you jumpy until you get used to it."

One day blended into the next—and the men became

146

accustomed to the noises. Tom commented they seemed a lot like the groanings and complainings of a bitter old woman.

Consciously Alton recalled what his friend had said about the power of God. Tom had said fear was not from God, hadn't he? A strange sense of peace stole over Alton. Peculiar. He'd not felt so calm before—not even under the blue skies in the clean, fresh out-of-doors.

Alton and Tom performed so well together as a team that it was a rare thing when a third man was assigned to work with them. Day after day the two of them labored in the old tunnel, chipping, chipping endlessly, as they filled car after car of coal to be hauled to the surface. Aged timbers creaked. Dust fell from the walls. But they paid no mind.

When one or the other took the cars up to be dumped, he'd cast an anxious eye to the weather. There looked to be no change in sight. Rain drummed upon the earth until mud was ankle-deep in the streets and still it continued to pour. Some of the old-timers remarked that it was the wettest spring in memory.

"There's no sense thinkin' about the farm in weather like this," Tom said, sighing. "If it doesn't clear soon, I can forget about farmin' for this year."

"I've been wishin' it'd stop myself," Alton said. "As soon as you leave, Preacher Tom, so do I."

"You wouldn't be goin' my way, now, would you?" Tom asked hopefully. "Sadie'd be honored to have you stay with us a spell, and the young'uns would love to have another man to call 'Uncle'."

"Well, I was kind of thinkin' 'bout it. Vandalia's 'tween here 'n' Effingham County. I was kind of hankerin' to go see Sue Ellen and Jem. Mebbe we could go together as far as your place. I could visit a short spell, meet the kinfolk, then travel on."

147

"I'd like that," Tom said. "Kind of thought you might be goin' to see the Stones."

The men settled back to their work, each caught up in his own private thoughts. A rumble, faint and far away, caused them to glance at each other with concern.

"Thunder?" Tom whispered questioningly.

"Well, either that . . . or a pocket of swamp gas explodin'," Alton murmured. His mind clutched at the first idea. "Prob'ly thunder," he said in a hearty tone. "Got to be! I saw storm clouds comin' up fast when I emptied the carts last."

The men returned to their work, speaking little, as their ears strained to catch the sound of further rumblings. Alton was just beginning to relax when he felt a faint vibration beneath his feet. He thought it was a product of his nervousness until he caught Tom's quick glance of alarm. It hadn't been his imagination. The earth had swayed under his feet.

"You felt it, too!" Alton whispered.

Tom nodded, seemingly calm, except for the widening of his eyes that were riveted on Alton's face. As the two men stared, a trickle of dirt pattered to the cavern floor.

"Oh, Lord!" Tom whispered, almost in prayer.

A timber creaked. In unison the men whirled. Their head lamps flitted and flashed, seeking out the weakening foundation.

Light, powdery dust hung in the air. The shaft of wood arched in the tunnel between them and freedom. When it creaked again, Tom leaped to life and sprinted forward. Alton stood, rooted to the ground.

"Alton, run!" Tom screamed.

Throwing himself against the aged timber, the young man clenched his teeth in a grimace of pain and determination. The offending screech of bending wood suddenly ceased.

"Run, Alton. Run for your life!"

Alton slowly came out of his dazed stupor.

"Run? Are you out of your mind, Tommy? *You* skedaddle!"

In two giant strides Alton had spanned the distance and was trying to wedge Tom aside to exert his greater bulk, but the slim miner refused to budge. Sweat beaded on Tom's brow as he leaned into the timber, shaking with the force of his exertion.

"Please, Alton!" Tom's voice trembled. "I can't hold it much longer. Go!"

"No!" Alton bellowed. "I ain't movin'—*you* are!"

"Alton, please!" Tom choked, straining, sobbing with frustration. "Would you please go?"

"No! You've got ever'thing to live for, Tom. I've got nothin'. No one will mourn me. Scat, you cheeky young pup!"

Tom's eyes clouded with tears. "I've never asked anything of you, Alton. Now I'm beggin'. Let me see you run to safety. It's my last request." Tom groaned, crying out to God as the timber moved almost imperceptibly.

"Tommy you—you don't know what you're doin', boy—," Alton whimpered. Alton felt as if he were being drawn away even as he wanted to cling for dear life.

"I do know what I'm doin'. You've got Sue Ellen. Jem. Your life ahead. You need one thing. Time. God willin', Alton, I can give you that. You're not right with the Lord, Alton. I'm better prepared to meet Him. You've given me so much. Let me give you one last thing—your life. Live on and look for God's plan before it's too late!"

"Tom!"

"Go," Tom choked. "Please!"

Shaken, Alton bolted, running with ragged steps. It was as if a force greater than he had scooped him up to catapult him ahead. Alton recognized the instant Tom attempted to spring free and follow him up the tunnel to safety. Alton covered his ears, but he would always hear the loud snap of the buckling timber before it sheared, followed by a thin, wavering scream that was quickly cut short by the roar of rock and dirt.

Alton ran like one possessed. Terror filled his heart. He lunged toward the surface, all the while expecting the earth to close in on top of him. Alton was faint with fright, trapped in a never-ending nightmare as demonic shadows moved each time he sought them in his light.

Out of breath, tripping, stumbling, staggering, Alton made his way out of the mine. He fell to the soggy ground, exhausted, tears coursing down his cheeks. Raindrops spattered on his broad back. Great sobs ripped from his chest.

Miners rushed to Alton's side.

"How many were with you?" an official asked in a grim tone.

Dully Alton turned over and faced him. "One. Just one—"

"Are you sure he's dead?" The question was gentle.

In his memory Alton heard the thin scream, the roar of the avalanche.

Alton turned to meet the man's eyes. As he did, dark storm clouds parted to reveal a ray of golden light that cleaved the heavens.

"Yes," Alton said quietly. "Tom McPherson died so I could live."

On the way to his shack, Alton's steps were heavy. Each footfall seemed a chanting cadence: live, live, live, *live!*

He would live. Tom had died for him, as Christ had died for everyone who would accept His sacrifice. Tom would not die in vain, for Alton knew now that he would live the rest of his life to the fullest, seeking the Lord's will, discovering the purpose of this life. He would return to Sue Ellen—clean—

not just washed up from the grime of the mine but clean inside. He would strive to become the man the Lord intended him to be. He, Alton Wheeler, would live on to find and serve the purpose for which he had been born.

The next morning the sky was leaden, but no rain fell. The sun peeked from behind scudding clouds, racing before a stiff breeze. A somber knot of roughly clothed miners stood at the mouth of the shaft Tom had entered, never to reappear.

The pastor from town arrived to perform the painfully short service. He said a prayer, then addressed the crowd.

"Greater love hath no man than to lay down his life for another."

The pastor extolled Tom's virtues as related to him by the young miner's friends. Another short prayer and the service was over. Miners shuffled back to their labor. It was just another day.

But for Alton, the day of Tom McPherson's funeral heralded new life, a new beginning.

chapter
11

EARLY THE NEXT morning Alton drove his team to the nearby town where he had deposited his money in the local bank. When he made his withdrawal, he separated his money from the cash he planned to take to Tom's widow along with Tom's personal possessions.

Guiding the horses down the road toward St. Louis, Alton thought about his future. When he had talked it over with Tom, the idea of going to see Sue Ellen had been an appealing one. Now, with the freedom to follow through, Alton wasn't at all sure Sue Ellen would be as glad to see him as he would be to feast his eyes on her. What if she'd married someone else? Or simply had no desire to see him?

He'd dwelt on happy memories for so long. Now, as he relived their last hours together, doubts returned to shake his confidence.

The horses covered the miles. Alton was aware of little but his sobering thoughts and a slithery sensation crawling around at the base of his stomach, combined with unbearable warmth.

He didn't know if the heat originated with the sudden sunshine that had chased the clouds away, or from his shame in remembering the cruel things he'd bellowed after Sue Ellen.

Alton fanned his cheeks, shucked his coat, and unbuttoned his faded shirt. Yet, still, the relentless heat persisted.

He arrived at the livery stable and bedded down his horses, then walked toward the nearby Idle Hour to get a room in the hotel. On the way, he swayed dizzily, braced himself against a lamppost, and swallowed hard as his stomach churned violently. Sweat popped out to bead his brow. A chill tingled through him. With ragged steps he made his way to the hotel. No one was at the desk, so he staggered into the saloon.

Archie was busy shining glasses. Barroom girls hovered solicitously near customers. The men engaged in a poker game played on, paying Alton no heed. Looking up, the bartender, seeing the way Alton was swaying, mistook him for a drunk.

"Need somethin', bub?" he asked.

"A room." Alton steadied himself against the bar.

Archie gave him a stern look. "Can you pay for it?"

"I've got money."

"Let's see the color of it," the bartender insisted. Alton peeled off a bill and slapped it on the bar. The barkeeper, seeing more where it came from, grew brusquely efficient.

"Audry! Got a feller here that's needin' to sleep one off. Take him upstairs and give him a room!" The bartender winked at the girl. She approached seductively, moistening her ruby lips as she curved her mouth into a generous smile.

"Take your time, sweetie," Archie whispered to her. "Business is slow. We won't need you down here for a while. See to it the bloke gets anything he wants—'n' charge him accordingly."

Audry pursed her lips and winked in agreement. "Come on, mister!" she purred and widened her grin when she felt the bulge of money in Alton's pocket. She put her arm around him to support him and clasped the room key in her other hand. "Upsy-daisy, fella."

When Alton's head drooped forward, Audry felt his feverish face against her own and realized then that he wasn't drunk, but sick. Wrestling Alton up the stairs, she coaxed him one step at a time.

"We're almost up to the landin', mister. Just a little bit further and we'll get you to your room." She sighed. "If I'd known you wasn't feelin' too pert, I'd have gotten a room closer to the stairs, 'stead of one for privacy."

Alton moaned and leaned against the wall as Audry jiggled the key in the lock and swung the door open. He stumbled across the room and sprawled on the bed.

"Are you goin' to be all right, mister?" she asked worriedly.

Alton's teeth clattered uncontrollably as chills wracked his body, and he writhed with cramping pains.

Hesitantly Audry crossed the room and touched his brow. It was like fanning glowing embers. The man was burning up with fever.

Taking action, she filled the ewer and dropped a clean towel into the tepid water before wringing it out to soothe his forehead. Alton opened his eyes a mere crack to smile his thanks.

She stared into those eyes, hauntingly familiar, and frowned, knowing she'd met him before. He stared at her in return, his eyes clearing for an instant.

"Audry? Miss Audry?" he murmured. She applied a cool cloth to his brow, then wiped his cheeks with another.

"That feels so much better, ma'am. Thank you, " Alton whispered.

Miss Audry? Ma'am!?

"Alton!" she cried softly. She felt her face flush when she

glimpsed a look of pity or maybe disappointment in his gentle eyes.

"How're you doin' in there, Audry?" Archie yelled, beating on the door.

"D—Don't worry none about us, Archie. We're gettin' along just dandy. I'm takin' care of the gent. You go back down to the bar."

Archie uttered a coarse laugh. "Just keep the customers happy, dolly!"

Alton was out of his head with the raging fever. Audry loosened his shirt and bathed his broad chest. Still his fever rose. Alternately Alton shivered while Audry piled quilts on him, or thrashed and moaned as the sweat poured from his skin.

Hours later, while Alton was sleeping soundly, Audry left the room and descended the stairs thoughtfully.

At her approach Archie smirked.

"How much did you get off him, sweetie?" he asked. "That bumpkin's carryin' a wad."

Audry gave him a flat look. "Nothin'."

"What's takin' you so long?" he bawled impatiently. "Are you havin' trouble rollin' that drunk? If you are, say the word, honey, and you'll have help."

"Mr. Wheeler's not drunk—he's sick."

"That makes it all the easier!" Archie said.

"I won't take advantage of a sick man. 'Specially not Mr. Wheeler."

"You've done it before—now do it again!" Archie glared.

Audry lifted her chin. Her lip trembled. "I—I won't!"

The bartender narrowed his eyes in warning. The girl ducked as he took a step in her direction.

"I thought I had all the sass took out of you, wench, and

months ago," he snarled. "What's got into you that you're defyin' me and not doin' as you're told?"

"Th-This fella, he's a good man. A God-fearin' man," Audry found herself explaining. "He's not like the others. Mr. Wheeler—Alton—he's always treated me like a decent woman. Now you want me to rob a man who's never been anything but nice to me? I won't do it, Archie! I can't return his kindness with cheatin'. For once, Archie, I'm going to act like a good woman."

"That's all it would be, Audry—an *act!*"

Archie's words stung, but she drew herself up to her full height. "I'm goin' back up to Mr. Wheeler's room. Don't bother comin' up again, Archie. The room's paid for. The other girls can work the bar and customers. Alton needs me. I ain't leavin' him."

The barrel-chested barkeep folded his arms across his chest. His jowls shook with laughter.

"If you're smart, dolly, you'll trade your heart of gold for the greenbacks in that gent's pockets. Honor sells cheap when you find yourself out in the street hungry, with no place to go."

Audry gave Archie a cold stare and walked up the stairs, slipping the bolt into place when she closed the door behind her. She tiptoed to the bed, wringing out a cool cloth for Alton's forehead.

It was almost dawn when he shifted, moaned, and opened his eyes a crack. Audry arose from the chair where she'd been keeping her vigil throughout the night.

Alton stared at her as if he did not recognize her and found her in place of another whose presence he expected.

"You're—you're not Sue Ellen."

Audry smiled sadly. "No. I'm not. But I'd sure like to know her."

Alton turned his face to the wall. "What happened? Did—"

Audry cut short his painful question. "I stayed with you to bring your fever down, that's all," she replied lightly.

"That was right kind of you. "

"I couldn't leave you. You were awfully sick."

"I don't remember much of anythin' about yesterday," Alton said thickly.

The day before seemed all of a decade ago. Tom's funeral. The bank. The trip to St. Louis.

"My horses!" Alton sat bolt upright, cold sweat pouring from his brow.

Audry touched his shoulder, easing him back to the pillow. "All taken care of," she soothed. "They're at the livery stable. I'll attend to them this morning and go tomorrow to pay for another day if need be."

"I'm much obliged, ma'am," he said weakly.

"Last night I doubted that you'd make it through the night, but you seem better today."

"I *am* better." Alton winced as he sat up. "I must've said plenty, not knowin' where I was . . . or who I was with."

Audry shrugged. "You ain't said nothin' to me this time, in your fever, that you didn't say months ago in rage and hurt." She flushed under Alton's appraising look, knowing that she had changed so much since they had last met that he had almost failed to recognize her. "You said enough to convince me you'll never have peace of mind nor happiness until you go see this Sue Ellen."

"I talked about Sue a lot?"

Audry lowered her gaze, nodding. "Sue Ellen Stone is a lucky woman, Alton," she said softly.

"She might not think so. Once I asked her to marry me. I still want her fer my wife. I know she loved me then. But what if she don't now?"

158

"Of course she loves you! Every woman dreams of findin' a man who'll love her the way you care for this Sue Ellen. I'm tellin' you true, go to her . . . 'n' you'll find out I'm right."

"How can you be so sure?" he asked doubtfully.

Audry's eyes were sad and distant. "I'm a woman, Alton. One who's lonely even when the saloon is crowded. A lot of men have wanted me, but no man has ever loved me. I—I'd die for the kind of love you have for Sue Ellen," she whispered. Her voice trembled with pain. "A woman would be a fool not to accept a love like yours. I'm a woman. That's how I know."

Her eyes brimming with tears, Audry left the room. Alton stared after her, wide-eyed. Could he dare hope she was right?

Thinking was an exhausting effort. Weakly Alton closed his eyes and dozed. But not before he vowed he would see Sue Ellen—at least once more.

Audry's face was lined with weariness when she descended the stairs to the saloon, brushing away the quick tears that flooded her eyes.

"Did you get the money from that bloke?" Archie spoke gruffly from behind her. Audry jumped, whirling.

"Yes!" she snapped.

Archie grinned, satisfied. "How much?"

Audry gave him a defiant smile. "Enough to take to the livery stable to pay for the keep of his horses."

The barkeep was outraged. "All the jack he's carryin', and that's all you're goin' to take from him?" He squinted. "You're gettin' a mite too independent, Audry. It's startin' to taint the other girls. I vow, wench, I won't tolerate such cheek. Mend your ways, fast, or you'll sure as shootin' find yourself turned out in the street. Maybe then you'll learn your place in the world."

"You can't turn me out in the street, Archie Bannister, because I'm quittin'!"

"Quittin'?"

"Right now!"

Archie rocked back on his heels, his arms folded across his barrel chest. "Go ahead," he invited. "By nightfall you'll be back, beggin' me to take you in."

"Don't hold your breath while you wait!" she warned. "Some of the things Alton Wheeler said last night when he was out of his head with a fever made more sense than what most folks say when they're sober."

Archie muttered a stream of oaths. "You're touched in the head, Audry, thinkin' you can go and be what you ain't."

Audry shrugged. "Maybe you think I'm only a trashy trollop, Archie. But Alton's always treated me with kindness. He gave me respect when no one else did. He made me believe that no one can force me to be bad. That I am what I am through my own choosin'. After listenin' to him, I know I want to change—and I will."

"Sure you will," Archie agreed sarcastically.

"I will!" Audry vowed. "I'm tired of bein' the kind of woman the world . . . men . . . expect me to be. From now on, I hope to be the kind of woman the Good Lord wants me to be."

"The Good Lord?" Archie bent double with laughter. "Well, if that don't beat all. And just what does a bawdy lady like you know about Him?"

Remembering, Audry's voice was soft. "A great deal more'n you might think. After Ma and Pa died, Gran took me in. We went to church and read the Good Book. If Gran hadn't died, things might've turned out different. If I hadn't felt that the Lord abandoned me, if I hadn't forgot that He'd provide for me 'n' watch out for me, I might not have decided to ... provide for myself by workin' in a place like this!"

When she left, Archie was still laughing, no doubt anticipating the ridicule of the Idle Hour customers when they heard Audry's news.

After she paid for the horses' keep, Audry took a hot meal to Alton's room. He awakened to the aroma of fresh coffee. Easing himself to a sitting position, he contemplated the food. At Audry's urging he took the first bite, then consumed the rest hungrily.

"You oughta rest today," she suggested.

Alton nodded. "I feel too weak to drag a dead cat."

"What are your plans?" Audry asked boldly.

"I'm goin' East. To Sue Ellen."

Audry folded her hands together in her lap, chewed her lip, took a deep breath and lifted her eyes. "I—I hate to trouble you, and I wouldn't, 'cept that I'm desperate. Mr. Wheeler, would you have room to take me along as far as Vandalia? I—I can't afford to pay much 'cause I'll need every bit of money I have to tide me over till I can find work."

"Don't want no pay a'tall," Alton said quietly. "I'll be ferever indebted to you fer takin' care of me. I'll take you along. And be right proud to have your company, too."

Audry's face brightened. "Thanks," she whispered as her voice trembled with new hope. "And, thank God!"

"We'll leave first thing in the mornin'," Alton promised, sensing her eagerness. "I'll be waitin' when dawn brings a new day."

To Archie's amazement and indignation, Audry made good her claim. She was packed and waiting when Alton came by with his wagon. Curious onlookers stared as Alton hefted her trunk to the wagon bed and helped her up to begin the journey. Alton squeezed her hand, then clambered up beside her.

"You look right pretty, Miss Audry. You look, well, like you did last year. Wouldn't have had no trouble recognizin' you the other day if you'd have looked like you do now."

Audry smiled. Her face was devoid of paint, her hair was arranged in a soft style, and she wore one of the girlish frocks that had been packed away since she'd arrived in St. Louis. The daring, sophisticated dresses she'd worn in the saloon had made her look like a woman of the world and concealed the fact that she was a scared young girl at heart.

Talk between them came easy. Alton pondered the fact that he was beginning to sound for all the world like Preacher Tom when answering Audry's eager questions.

The first night out, the sky was clear and flecked with stars. Instead of spending money on a hotel, they camped along the road. Alton fixed Audry a place on the wagon. After the embers died low, Alton nestled against the trunk of a thick cottonwood tree and dozed until twittering birds and the sun's first rays awakened him.

Two more days on the road brought them nearer Audry's hometown and gave her pale skin a healthy golden glow.

Alton couldn't help noticing that Audry tensed as they drew near Vandalia in the late afternoon of the fourth day. He smiled at her excitement as she pointed out familiar landmarks and sympathized with the anxiety she felt at the prospect of returning after so many months.

"Here we are, Audry," Alton said softly. "Whoa!" Alton halted the team on the town's main street in front of a neat hotel.

"Thanks for bringin' me, Alton."

"Glad to help out. And I wish you nothin' but the best."

"The best is what I'm goin' to find here," Audry said

confidently. "There are bound to be a few folks who'll gossip about the kind of woman I was when I went to St. Louis last year. But there are good people here, too—forgivin' people. They're people who'll remember Gran with kindness, and, I hope," she swallowed hard, "allow me the same."

Alton squeezed her hand and smiled until his eyes crinkled. "Sure they will," he promised. "Lookin' at you, Audry, ain't no one would guess at the life you put behind you, 'lessen you tell 'em. You're startin' over all clean. It's not people's opinions that matter, remember that. Only the Lord's opinion counts."

"I'm in your debt, Alton, for makin' me believe in myself again. And in showin' me the way, and helpin' me get there. I'll make someone such a fine housekeeper there'll be no regrets for givin' me a second chance. You'll be proud of me, Alton," she promised.

"Already am," he murmured. "Takes courage to find a new life and rely on the Good Lord to provide. He will, though. Don't you doubt it for a minute."

Alton lugged Audry's trunk into the hotel lobby. He turned, extended his hand, and Audry took it. Tears filled her eyes.

"I hope we meet again someday," she whispered.

"Lord willin', Miss Audry, I'm sure we will."

Audry stood on tiptoe and brushed a quick kiss across his bearded cheek. "Now get along with you," she said, "or you'll leave me cryin' in the street."

Alton shuffled, staring at the ground as he fingered the wad of bills in his pocket. A moment later he pressed them into Audry's hand.

Her eyes sharpened with pain. "No, Alton! Don't ruin things by tryin' to *pay* me!"

"I'm not payin' you for caring for me. I'm givin' you a gift.

You're my friend. Startin' out brand-new like you are, I just want to make things easier till you land yerself a job. Sort of a goin'-away present."

Audry thought it over. "In that case, I'll accept it—with my thanks."

"It's the least I can do," Alton explained softly. "After all, you had a chance to take all of my money, and Tom McPherson's, too—and you didn't."

"Pray for me, Alton."

"I will," he murmured. "And when you speak with the Lord yerself, kindly make mention of me 'n' mine."

Alton squeezed by, then he was gone.

Tom had described the road to his place so many times that Alton felt he'd have been able to find it in the dark with his eyes closed.

He reined in Doc and Dan when he saw the lane that he knew led to the cabin in the woods where Tom's widow lived with her brother and the young'uns. He considered—and rejected—a thousand words. How, *how* was he going to break the news to Sadie McPherson that her Tom was dead?

The realization was like a dull ache that filled Alton's entire being. He'd known and loved Tom for only a few months. What would the agony be for the woman who'd loved him for so long and borne his children? Surely no words could describe it—nor relieve it.

Praying for strength and wisdom, Alton halted in the McPherson yard near the neat cabin, built solid and strong like Tom himself.

A little child, probably Katie, looked at him with large, troubled eyes.

"Is your mama here, honey?"

Nodding, her braids flapping, she turned to fetch her mother.

"Sadie," he said when she appeared in the cabin door.

"Mr. Wheeler! Alton," she whispered. She bit her lip. Her eyes, red from crying, filled again. She hurried to him and took his hand in hers. "I knew you'd be comin'. Tom told me I could count on you." She paused and wiped a tear. "I—I got the telegram from the coal company the day after it happened. I've been lookin' for you ever since."

Alton wrung his hat. "You'll never know how sorry I am, Miz Sadie."

She nodded and led the way to the house. "Guess I do," she corrected. "Tom loved you like a brother. And I know you felt the same. You were with him those last days, Alton. It'd ease my grief a great deal if you'd share those times with me, so's in your memories, at least, I can make 'em my own."

Alton and Sadie talked on for hours—laughing, crying, falling silent, praying. He ate with the family, noticing the faith that bound them together, the belief that made them bear sadness with happy hope found only in Christ.

After the children said their prayers, Sadie's brother read a book, and Sadie took an oil lamp to the table and beckoned Alton to join her.

He sat down, accepted the cup of hot coffee, and looked at her expectantly.

"What are your plans now, Alton?" she asked. "You're welcome to stay on and visit here, like Tom always wanted—"

"I'm goin' to see some friends—Miz Stone and her boy, Jem, over in Effingham County."

A smile flitted briefly, erasing some of the grief etched in Sadie's features.

"Alton, I'm so happy! I've been prayin' about that ever

165

since Tom asked me to remember you both when I talk with the Lord."

"You—you've been prayin'—fer me?" he asked, incredulously. "And Sue Ellen?"

She nodded. "It's going to work out, Alton," Sadie said with confidence. "I can just feel it in my heart. Tom, he told me a bit about you and what he suspected about Sue Ellen."

Alton told Sadie the rest.

Sadie smiled. "In her place, Alton, I'd have turned you down then, too. But if it was me, I wouldn't turn down the man you are now. And neither will Sue Ellen."

chapter
12

ALTON MADE RECORD time after leaving Sadie McPherson's farm with promises to stop in the very next time he passed by.

When he entered Effingham, he made his way to the general store to purchase a few supplies. Behind the counter was the clerk who'd sold him the green ribbon so many months before. He greeted Alton as if it had been only days since he'd seen him last.

"Has Miz Stone from the Salt Creek area been in lately?" asked Alton. "A widow woman with a boy?"

"Oh, I know the lady, but it's been a while since I've seen her," the clerk replied. "Quite a spell, come to think of it." He jotted some figures on a piece of paper. "Miz Stone must be about due to come into town, though now that you mention it, I haven't seen her since the cholera epidemic."

Alton hurriedly paid for his purchases and left Effingham for the Salt Creek community. Fearing for Sue Ellen's safety, he made better time than he figured. The horses, too, seemed to sense his urgency and champed at the bit restlessly whenever Alton attempted to rein them in.

Presently he forded Salt Creek, passed Will and Fanny's farm, and no longer tried to curb the horses. Instead, he gave them their heads and they hurtled for home. Alton slowed the team only to negotiate the familiar lane leading to Sue Ellen's place.

As they approached the cabin, he regarded it warily. Though it was noon, no smoke curled from the chimney to signal that Sue Ellen was preparing a meal. Doc and Dan snorted and stomped, but no one came to the door to investigate the noise. The windows of the cabin stared blankly, like the vacant eyes of a bleached skull.

"Ho—o! Anyone home?" Alton called.

He left the wagon and knocked on the door, but the cabin remained ominously still.

Birds twittered overhead, objecting to his intrusion. Alton cocked his head. Far away, down in the bottom, he heard the steady *chunk, chunk* of an ax biting wood.

Jem!

Alton's pulse quickened. No doubt the boy and his mother had gone to the woods, perhaps with a picnic lunch. Alton turned the horses into the pasture and crossed to the timber.

Shirtless, Jem was slinging the ax again and again, his muscles rippling with the exertion. The boy, now grown taller and tanned, mopped his brow on his forearm. When the big hickory toppled, it shook the earth beneath Alton's feet, causing it to shudder with the impact.

Alton called out before the next stroke fell, and Jem whirled, startled. He broke into a grin, threw down the ax, and ran to greet Alton. The older man grabbed the boy close against him.

"Alton, I can't believe it's you! Mama said you'd be back."

"I looked for your mama, Jem. Where is she?"

Jem brushed the hair from his eyes and chewed his lip, manfully trying to control his emotions. Seeing the glow of tears in Jem's eyes and observing his struggle, Alton was alarmed.

"Where *is* your mama, boy. Answer me!"

"She's gone."

"*Gone?!*"

The word ripped from Alton's throat. He reeled from the vision of quick death to cholera that had snaked through his mind so many times to coil in the pit of his stomach. Alton slumped to a nearby stump, his face pale.

"Gone." Despairingly Alton dropped his head to his hands.

Jem saw the grief and understood. "Mama's not dead, Alton. She's just over to the Bridger farm for a few days. Miz Bridger, she's birthin'. Jesse came by and got Mama. The baby was born yesterday, Will said, so Mama'll probably be home sometime today."

Relief flooded Alton's eyes. "I thought you meant she'd been taken by the cholera, boy. Plumb scared me to death."

"We lost a few people in the neighborhood, sure enough, but we were pretty lucky. Ma'll sure be glad to see you, Alton. She worried constantly that you'd catch the plague and die. Mama missed you somethin' awful. We both have—"

"No more than I missed you two," Alton murmured. "I'm sorry I left without botherin' to say good-bye to you, son. I guess you know I was hurtin' . . . 'n' why." Jem nodded. "Your ma was dead right in turnin' me down. Lookin' back, I can see I wasn't the man for her then. I hope and pray I am now."

Jem leaned on the handle of the ax worn smooth from use. "That's been Mama's prayer, too. She hasn't been the same since you left. Sometimes I'd catch her lookin' down the lane like she was waitin' for you to drive the team in. Mama never lost her love or her faith . . . in God or in you. She said you'd be back when the time was right."

"Thanks be to the Good Lord, I'm here now." Alton's voice was husky. "I think you'll both be glad to hear that He's my

Lord, too." Alton leaned back on the large stump and surveyed the clearing. "You've done a good job, Jem, but you could use some help."

Alton reached for Jeremiah's ax that had fallen to the ground.

"Don't! Stop!" Jem cried. He sprang ahead.

Puzzled by the outcry, Alton turned to look at Jem, groping for the ax handle among the leaves with his right hand. Then, following the boy's horrified gaze, he tried to check his movement. But it was too late.

Alton's eyes widened when he saw the dead leaves move and witnessed the thick body uncoil, rising up, up, mouth gaping, sharp fangs long and curving. The rattler's tail whirred. His mouth yawned even wider. Drops of venom formed on the fangs.

"Alton!" Jem screamed. He tried to shove Alton out of the rattler's reach, but the man's motion worked counter to Jem's attempt.

The snake, feisty after the winter season, sprang. Milky venom squirted through the air before the curved fangs, sharp as needles, sank into the flesh of the man's upper arm and set his skin afire.

"Oh, God—"

Alton's horrified murmur became a moan of terror. He jumped up, frantically trying to shake the rattlesnake loose. The rattler hung on, twisting and writhing, dangling from his arm. A dull, heavy sensation replaced the searing pain.

It seemed an eternity although it was only moments before the snake dropped off and began to slither away. Jem swung the ax in a chopping motion, again and again, but the blade bit into the ground, and the snake slithered away under the leaves. Frantically Jem hurled the ax. Cut in half, the rattlesnake twisted back on itself, curling and knotting in spasms of death.

Jem ran back to Alton. He sat on the stump, shaking, clutching his arm.

"What do I do?" Jem asked. "What do I do?"

"Stay calm," Alton murmured, fighting his own panic. He forced himself to breathe slowly. "Take my knife." Alton reached into his pocket with his good arm and withdrew the blade.

"Cut into the center of each fang mark, boy. We've got to get the poison out."

Alton tugged at his thick leather belt, then wrapped it around his arm, jerking it so tightly that the metal buckle bit into the pale flesh of his underarm.

Jem winced when Alton sliced into his flesh to deepen the wound. Alton lowered his lips to the wound, then spat blood into the bed of curling brown leaves that littered the forest floor.

"Let me, Alton. You're weakening too fast."

Again and again Jem emptied the wound and spat the poisons on the ground. When he finally stopped for breath, he eyed Alton anxiously.

"We've got to get help. Get you to the cabin."

"Lord willin', I'll make it, Jeremiah," he said weakly. "I can't believe the Good Lord would bring me this far fer no reason."

"Ma should be home soon. She'll know what to do."

"Help me, Jem." Alton stood up, reeling, and pitched forward, almost falling before Jem caught him.

Jem braced the big man, wriggling into place to support Alton with his own height and strength. Each step up the hills to the cabin in the clearing was a victory. When Jem saw Sue

Ellen by the cistern, he was so winded he could scarcely breathe.

"Ma!" cried Jem. The word came out a faint bleat and was carried away by the stirring wind. "*Ma-a-a-a-a-a!*"

Sue Ellen turned. Her mouth dropped open when she looked toward the barn, saw the team and wagon there, and searched beyond to find Jem and Alton emerging from the woods. Clutching up her skirts, she rushed across the space that separated them.

"Alton! What happened, Jem?"

"A snake," he panted. "A timber rattler. As big around as my arm."

"Did you—?"

Then Sue Ellen saw the thick belt already disappearing into the swelling mass of Alton's upper arm. The knife slashes gaped wide from the puffing skin.

"We did what we could, Ma. Now what?"

Sue Ellen looked at the wound, saw Alton's dazed state, his staggering weakness. She swallowed hard.

"Pray."

Together they got Alton to the cabin. Sue Ellen cut away the shirt sleeve with a flash of her shears. Alton lay on her bed, his skin pallid, his breath jerky and faint, his movements lifeless.

"Is he goin' to die, Ma?"

"Not if I can help it!" she said, eyes flashing. "I don't know much about treating snakebites, but with the grace of God, he'll pull through."

"I'll ride for Doc Wiggins," Jem said. "I'll unhitch Dan and leave right away."

"Godspeed, son," Sue Ellen whispered.

Jem was gone before he heard her speak.

Alton spent a harrowing afternoon. His skin became cold and clammy, and his breath was so shallow that Sue Ellen had to hold her face close to his to assure herself that he was still alive. Time and again she brewed the herbs Fanny had given her and forced the healing fluid down his throat, drop by precious drop.

At dusk Sue Ellen heard the sound of hooves clattering on the path. But when she looked out it was only Jem, astride Dan's broad back. There was no sign of Dr. Wiggins' black carriage.

"Where's the doctor?" she asked Jem as he hurried into the house.

"He couldn't come," Jem explained in a rush. "I spoke with his housekeeper. She said he left to tend a woman over near Eberle. She's been in labor three days, 'n' the housekeeper said Doc can't leave her."

Quietly they entered the room where Alton lay.

"Will he be all right, Ma?"

"I don't know. We've done the best we can. The Lord will have to do the rest."

Sue Ellen was up throughout the night, coaxing herb teas down Alton, then clear broth. Come morning, Jem found his Ma keeping vigil in her rocking chair.

"How is he?"

"Still sleeping."

When Alton heard Jem's voice, he weakly called to him. With a questioning look at his mother, Jem entered the room.

"I'm here, sir," he said and stood beside the bed.

"Alone, Jem."

Reluctantly Sue Ellen left the room.

"We're alone now, Alton."

The big man gestured Jem closer.

"Go for the preacher, son. *Now!* Don't waste any time."

173

"You're—you're sure?" Jem whispered.

Alton's eyes closed. "Never more sure of anything in my life." A peaceful smile curved his lips.

"I'll go right away."

Jem left the room to confront Sue Ellen's green eyes that were large with worry and unspoken questions.

"I'm ridin' for the preacher, Ma. Alton asked me to fetch him. He's a Christian now, Ma," Jem tried to comfort her. "Earlier he was talkin' about the Lord 'n' all—but I better go now."

Silently Sue Ellen watched Jem leave. Her face crumpled. Brokenhearted, she buried her face in her arms and sobbed. Then she prayed as she'd never prayed before.

"Thank You, oh, thank You for changing Alton's heart! If he can't be with me, I'm just so glad he'll be with You!" she cried. "But You know how much I want Alton to live, how much Jem and I love him, and I'd count it a favor if You'd see fit to spare him just a little longer—but Thy will, not mine, be done," she whispered.

Alton's voice was faint, so faint at first that Sue Ellen didn't hear him call. Quickly she brushed the tears from her eyes and entered the room. Alton motioned her to him. When she stood beside him, he took her hand and reached up to trace the line of her cheek and lip.

"I love you, Sue Ellen. Very much."

It was more than Sue Ellen could bear, having Alton vow his love as he lay a dying man. The tears she'd tried to contain spilled over.

"Alton, oh, Alton—"

Tears choked Sue Ellen's speech. She sank to her knees beside the bed and threw her arms around his neck.

Alton cradled her head to his chest, smoothing her dark hair beneath his palm. His chest grew damp from her tears.

"Jem's not back yet?"

She shook her head. "Is there something I can do to make you more comfortable until the preacher gets here?"

Alton managed a weak grin. "You might consider changin' into that green-and-white dress . . . the one I wanted you to be married in." He looked out the window. "It's lookin' to be a perfect day for a weddin'."

Sue Ellen stared into Alton's blue eyes and saw the glint of mischief there—the returning of strength.

"I sent Jem to get the preacher, not for buryin' but for marryin', girl. I've seen the answer in your eyes, Sue. Now let me hear it on your lips."

"Oh, Alton—"

"Please be my wife, Sue Ellen."

Tears of joy filled her eyes. "Yes! Oh my, yes!"

"While you're gettin' dressed, I'd better do somethin' to make myself presentable."

Sue Ellen opened the trunk and hugged the green dress to her before she left the room to put it on. She brushed her hair until it cascaded, dark and rich, around her creamy shoulders.

Sue Ellen heard the sound of horses. Looking out, she saw two riders trailing behind the pastor's carriage. Jem and . . . Will. And Fanny sitting beside the preacher.

Alton came out of the bedroom and stood behind Sue Ellen. Slipping his arms around her slim waist, he dropped a kiss on the soft nape of her neck. His own skin now felt cool to the touch.

"It's a perfect day for a weddin', ain't it?" he asked in a voice husky with love and emotion.

"Just perfect," Sue Ellen sighed with contentment.

"There's only one thing missin' to make you the most beautiful bride ever."

Sue Ellen turned in the circle of his arms and lifted an inquiring eyebrow.

"And that would be?" she asked, the promise of fulfillment in her emerald eyes.

"When I asked you to marry me before, Sue, I told you my bride would wear green ribbons in her hair—ribbons the color of her eyes."

A sharp look of disappointment crossed Sue Ellen's face. "But I don't have any hair ribbons, Alton."

"Oh, but you do!"

Alton took out the ribbon he had carried for so long, folded away in the tissue paper in his tobacco pouch. Sue Ellen looked at it, and then she understood.

"So that's the item you simply had to go back into the general store to buy that day!" she whispered.

Alton nodded. "I've carried it in my pocket the way I've carried love in my heart, Sue Ellen, ever since the day I met you. That ribbon was meant for you. I wanted to give it to you several times, but somehow the moment was never right. Now it is. I give you the ribbon as I give you my promise to love you for as long as I live."

"I knew it would be like this someday," she sighed. "The Lord brought you back to me, Alton, in love's own time—"